CW00879666

KNOWING YOUR SEWING

This book has been planned as a textbook for CSE Needlework examinations, but could also provide useful revision material for GCE. The aim has been to advise on essential stages of dressmaking (including the very important basic decisions on garment, pattern and fabric) but at the same time not to overload the subject with confusing detail. To round things off, there is a helpful chapter on how to tackle the examination itself.

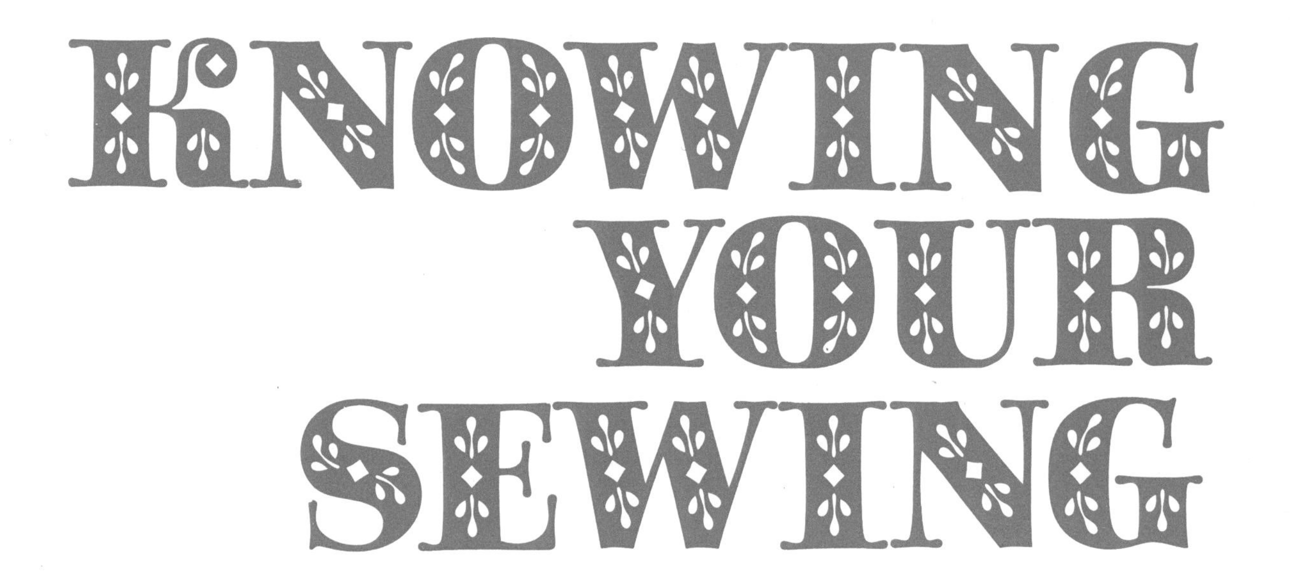

Maureen Goldsworthy, M.A.
Head of Needlework, Campion High School for Girls

Diagrams by Janet Watson

MILLS & BOON LIMITED, LONDON

First published 1972 by Mills & Boon Limited,
17–19 Foley Street, London W1A 1DR

Reprinted 1973

ISBN 0 263 05148

Printed in Great Britain by Butler & Tanner Ltd
Frome and London

CONTENTS

Note: In the diagrams throughout the book, shading has been used, where needed, to show the right side of the fabric, as in most well-known commercial patterns.

YOUR CLOTHES

PLANNING YOUR CLOTHES

Nobody can ever have as many clothes as they would like, so it is important to find out exactly what clothes you need, and **plan your wardrobe.**

First, put out on your bed **all** your clothes and accessories (bags, scarves, belts, etc.). Have a good look at them and divide them into three piles:

1. All your wearable clothes.
2. Anything that could be made wearable if it were altered or re-made into a different garment, (such as trousers into shorts).
3. Things that are now too small for you, or too old, or beyond hope. **Get rid of these** to someone who can use them—if only as dusters.

Now make a list of all the clothes and accessories that are left. This will help you see what goes together—what gaps there are—what you need most urgently—and how to plan your spending.

WHY MAKE YOUR CLOTHES?

1. You can get exactly what you want in fit, colour, material, style and fashion.
2. You can have "one-off" clothes, and be different.
3. You can make your money go much further and have more clothes—**or** have better-made clothes of better material than you could buy at the same price.
4. When you find how easy dress-making can be, you will have an enjoyable and life-long hobby.

WHICH CLOTHES TO MAKE AND WHICH TO BUY?

Do not make—Garments that are too thick or heavy for you to handle easily—such as thick coats.

Garments that are too difficult for your skill—choose simple patterns.

Garments that must fit perfectly, such as swim-wear, bra's and tight-fitting trousers.

Underwear, if it is cheaper to buy ready-made.

Do make—Skirts—easiest of all, and they save the most money.

Shorts, flared trousers.

Dresses, blouses, waistcoats and cardigans.

Accessories such as bags, belts, chokers, watch-straps—especially in suède, leather, felt, etc. You can save pounds.

QUALITY OR THROW-AWAY FASHION?

Spend as much as you can afford on

Your **winter coat**—you will wear it for more than half the year and it should last as "best" for two or three winters.
Really good well-fitting **shoes** with thick soles for work.

Really good fabric for woollen **skirts** that will not "seat" but keep their new look longer.

Buy as cheaply as you can

Summer tops and Tee-shirts—Tights—Party shoes and sandals—Fashion crazes that will be dead in a few weeks.

THE CLOTHES YOU WILL NEED—FOR THE LIFE YOU LEAD

At weekends you will need clothes for leisure—for out-of-doors—for evening dates.

When you leave school, where will you be working?

In a shop or factory? You will need blouses and skirts or trousers to wear under overalls—make all these, and save money for leisure clothes. You will need comfortable shoes.

In a Hospital, Women's Services, Police? Your shoes must be good, but you will be able to spend the rest of your money on off-duty clothes.

In an office or receptionist's job? You will need your own well-groomed working clothes—Easy dresses, jerseys, cardigans, blouses, skirts. Trousers if permitted.

Out of doors? Your first needs are a good waterproof and strong shoes or boots.

Do not forget the accessories—they can turn a collection of oddments into an outfit. Bag, scarf, belt, hat, gloves, tights, boots, shoes—any of these can help to give you an all-over fashion look.

CLOTHES THAT MATCH OR MIX

Unless you have plenty of money to spend, keep your clothes and accessories to one colour range for winter, and one for summer. You may already have brown shoes, a navy coat and a black handbag—these do not mix well, but if you stick to **one basic colour range** in all your future buying, you will soon match-or-mix. Here are some colour ranges—or think out your own.

With navy or grey Purple, plum, pink, all the blues, yellow, orange, red, pale green, beige, white.

With brown Orange, rust, plum, all the greens, pale blue, turquoise, yellow, salmon, beige, cream.

With black Reds, emerald or pale green, tan, orange, yellow, royal or pale blue, camel, pink, mauve, white.

With plum or purple Blues, pinks, mauves, black, pale yellow, beige.

With beige or camel Almost everything except greyish blues.

WHAT SHOULD YOUR CLOTHES DO FOR YOU?

As well as being fashionable, and suitable for the times when you wear them, clothes should make you look your best.

Colours should flatter your skin, hair or eyes. Look again at the colour ranges—the colours that go with navy are good for girls with blonde or light brown hair, fair skins, and blue or grey eyes. Medium brunettes or redheads would be better with the warmer colours in the brown range, while girls with olive skins or very dark colouring would look best in the brilliant colours that go with black. Plum and purple are best on fair-skinned people, and almost anyone **except** fair girls can wear the beige and camel range. You are lucky if you have in-between colouring, for then you can look well in any colour. But work out your **own** list of colours—what **you** like is most likely to suit you.

Styles can help your figure.

Look slimmer with wide collars or revers—puffed sleeves—or any wide shoulder line to make waist and hips look smaller. V-necklines or V-shaped yokes; or stripes, patterns or seams going up-and-down also make you look slimmer.

Look more curvy with gathers over the bust—unpressed pleats or gathers at hip level—big patch pockets—flared skirts—wide, tight belts.

Look taller with flared skirts—no belt or seam at the fitted waist (Princess Line)—skirt falling straight from a high bust-line (Empire Line). Wear the same colour above and below the waist, matching top to skirt or trousers. Trousers can make you look taller and more leggy—try tucking your shirt inside, for a longer leg line. Wear matching boots up to the skirt or gaucho level. Shoes cut low in front can also make your legs look longer.

Look shorter with belts and hip interest—stripes, seams or patterns going across the figure—large patch pockets—flounces or frills to break up the long line of a skirt—long belted tunics over trousers. High-fronted shoes can make legs look shorter.

Fabrics with a dull surface are more slimming than shiny ones; ciré or wet-look fabrics show every bulge and only the very slim can wear them—except as accessories. Leather and Vinyl (fake leather) can be slimming as they are warm without the bulk of woolly fabrics.

BUDGETING—PLANNING WHAT YOU SPEND

Try to save something **every week**, even while you are still at school. The secret is **regular saving**, not in a money-box at home, but with a Savings Bank Account, or at the Post Office, or in a Clothing Club. Save-as-you-go and pay-as-you-buy is the golden rule—it gives you more freedom of choice, and saves you from piling up debts you might not be able to pay off easily.

Get value for money by comparing prices—street markets are often much cheaper than shops, both for fabrics and for garments, but be sure to look carefully, as market stalls often sell "seconds".

Credit Buying means that you can have goods before they are fully paid for. This is useful if you have to buy many garments in a short time—but be sensible and do not have more credit than you can afford, as it all has to be paid for in the end.

Mail Order Catalogues usually let you pay over 20 weeks for goods you have had, without any extra charge.

Budget Accounts in fashion stores usually let you buy goods up to 8 to 10 times the amount you pay off each month. There is no extra charge.

Hire Purchase is more often used for household goods than for clothes. You pay an extra charge for the credit, and the goods do not belong to you until you have finished paying for them.

LABELLING IN GARMENTS

The label inside the neckline should show:

The maker's or brand name—a well-known name usually means good value.
The size—in very cheap garments, you may need a size larger than usual.
The material from which the garment is made, such as "Pure New Wool"; or the amounts of different fibres in a mixture, such as "55% Terylene and 45% Wool Worsted".
Washing or dry-cleaning instructions.

FINDING YOUR RIGHT SIZE

Measurements are the same as for paper patterns (page 28).

Size 10 for Bust 32″ (82 cm) and hips 34″ (87 cm).
Size 12 for Bust 34″ (87 cm) and hip 36″ (91 cm).
Size 14 for Bust 36″ (92 cm) and hip 38″ (97 cm).
Size 16 for Bust 38″ (97 cm) and hip 40″ (102 cm).

There are also special sizes for young styles in very short lengths:

Size 1 for 32″ Bust.
Size 2 for 34″ Bust.
Size 3 for 36″ Bust and
Size 4 for 38″ Bust.

CARING FOR YOUR CLOTHES

Never leave them on the floor in a heap.

Never put them away dirty, or wear them too long before washing.

Never put damp clothes away in polythene bags, or they will be mildewed.

Always brush garments, and hang them on hangers while they are still warm—this helps them to shed creases and keep their shape.

Always clean your shoes while still warm, bend them back into shape and stuff the toes with paper.
Always see that summer clothes are clean, mended and pressed before putting them away at the end of the season. Woollen clothes put away in the spring can be protected from moths if they are sealed **perfectly clean** into polythene bags.
Always see to shoe repairs and small mending jobs before they get worse.

QUICK REPAIRS

Emergency Kit Carry two needles in your bag, one threaded with white and one with black thread. You can then stitch loose buttons, split seams or fallen hems on the spot.

Darn thin places, such as sweater elbows, **before** they go into holes. **Machine darning** can be done on firm fabrics with a swing-needle machine, using a medium zig-zag stitch—or the 3-step zig-zag on an automatic machine. Run the stitching backwards and forwards over the thin place, then turn the darn and stitch at right angles backwards and forwards across the first stitching.

Invisible patching—Use Bondaweb or Bondina, a sticky plastic, spread on a paper backing.

For L-shaped tears. Cut a patch of fabric larger than the tear, and with the threads running in the same direction. Put a piece of Bondaweb or Bondina on the right side of the patch, paper side upwards, and iron it on with a warm iron. Allow it to cool. Peel off the paper backing, and the right side of the patch will now be sticky. Place this side to the **wrong** side of the tear, and press with a **steam** iron, or with an ordinary iron over a damp cloth. Leave to cool and set for 10 minutes.

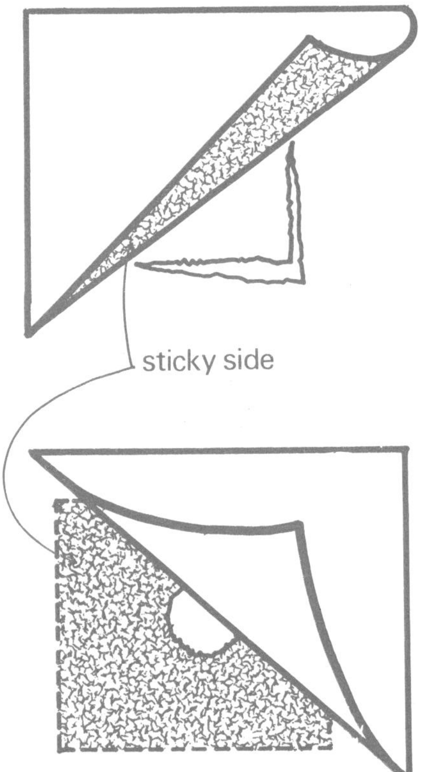

For Holes. Iron the Bondina or Bondaweb on to the **wrong** side of the garment itself, peel off the backing paper, cut away the sticky web across the hole, and place a fabric patch with its right side to the sticky wrong side of the garment. Press with a steam iron and leave to set. Trim off any loose edges on the wrong side.

WASHING CLOTHES

Most garments carry labels with these numbered instructions for different materials:

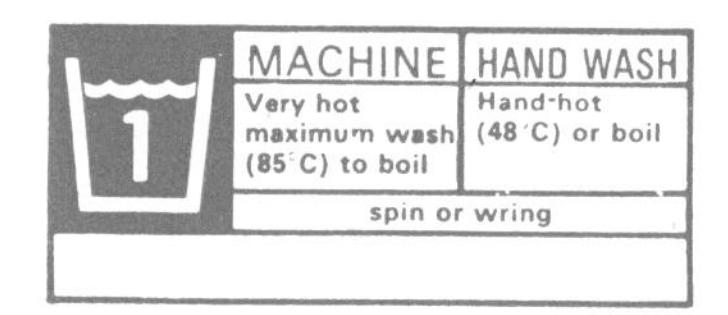

1. For white cotton and linen articles without special finishes.

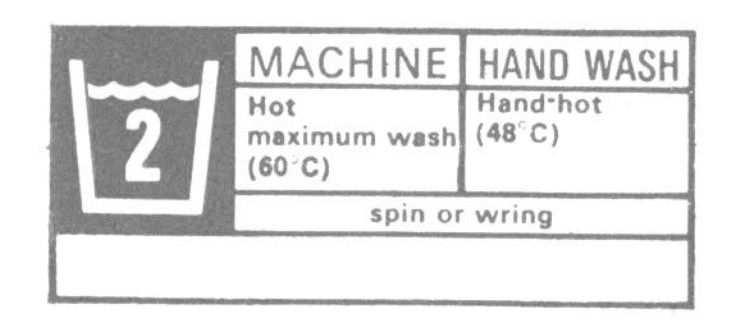

2. For cottons, linens or rayons without special finishes, where colours are fast at 60°C. (The colour-fast wash.)

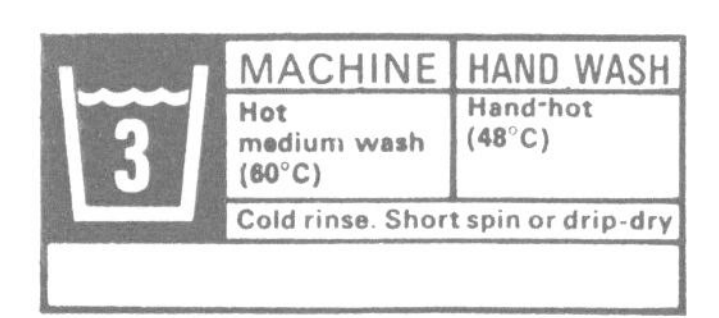

3. For white Nylon. (Do not tumble-dry, as this will cook in any creases. The cold rinse helps to avoid creases.)

4. Coloured Nylon, Terylene, Crimplene; cottons and rayons with special finishes (such as "easy-care", "minimum iron" or "drip-dry"); acrylic/cotton mixtures.

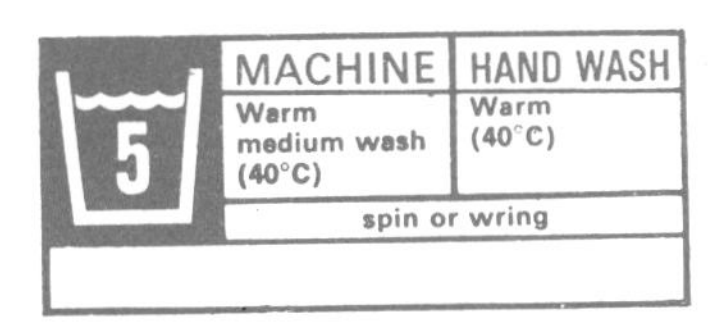

5. Cottons, linens or rayons where colours are fast at 40°C but not at 60°C.

6 MACHINE | HAND WASH
Warm minimum wash (40°C) | Warm (40°C)
Cold rinse. Short spin. Do not wring

6. Acrilan, Courtelle and Orlon; acetate and Tricel, including mixtures with wool; Terylene/wool blends.
(Dry knitted garments flat on a towel.)

7 MACHINE | HAND WASH
Warm minimum wash (40°C) | Warm (40°C) Do not rub
Spin. Do not hand wring

7. Wool, including blankets and wool mixtures with cotton or rayon. (Woollen garments should be rinsed at the **same** temperature as they are washed, to avoid shrinking. Roll in a towel, pull to shape and dry flat.)
Silk.

8 HAND WASH ONLY
WARM (40°C)
Warm rinse. Hand-hot final rinse. Drip dry

8. Washable pleated garments containing Acrilan, Courtelle, Orlon, Nylon, Terylene or Tricel.

See page 17 for more about man-made fibres.

IRONING

Different fabrics need different heat settings, shown on the iron:

1. Cool. For Acrylic fabrics (Acrilan, Orlon, Courtelle).
2. Warm. For acetate, Tricel, Nylon, polyesters (Terylene, Dacron, Crimplene), wool and silk.
3. Medium Hot. For viscose rayon (Sarille, Vincel).
4. Hot. For cotton and linen without special finishes.

Wool should be ironed with a steam iron or under a damp cloth.
Cotton and linen should be ironed damp, on the right side if a shiny finish is wanted.
Silk should be ironed on the wrong side while still evenly damp.
Man-made fibres must **never** be ironed damp.
Iron with long, smooth movements—do not press heavily; the heat does the work.

DRY CLEANING

(With a spirit cleaner instead of water.)

Dry cleaning is expensive, but it is far more expensive to ruin good tweed skirts, or soft crêpe dresses, by shrinking them in the wash. It is almost always safer to dry-clean woven wool—knitted wool of course is washable. Any garments, including suède and wet-look, can be dry-cleaned, (but **not** rubberised rain-wear).

Cautions: Plastic buttons should be removed as they may melt.
Dry-clean **before** dirt works deep into the fabric.

Dry-cleaning can be much cheaper if done by weight (usually in 8 lb loads) at a launderette. Remove spots and stains at home, and your clothes will need fewer cleanings.

REMOVING STAINS

First try soaking in plain cold water—hot water may cook in stains.
Then try rubbing with warm water and detergent.
New stains are easy to lift—**old** stains are much more difficult.

Greasy marks, Crayon stains Can be removed with spirit cleaners (Thawpit, Dabitoff, etc.)

Coffee, Tea, Blood, Egg, Ink Come out in cold, running water if treated at once.

Chewing Gum must first be rubbed with an ice cube to harden it. Then it can be scraped off with a blunt knife. Dissolve the rest of the mark with spirit cleaner. Rinse well.

Grass, Ball-point ink Difficult, but may come out with methylated or surgical spirit.

GOOD GROOMING

Looking your best is more than just clothes.

Your hair The first thing people notice about you, should be well cut and shaped. Wash it often. To make it shine, rinse with lemon juice if you are fair, with vinegar if you are dark, or with beer if you can stand the smell.

Your Skin Many young skins are greasy and spotty; they **will** improve with thorough cleansing **twice a day** with soap-and-water or cleansing milk (**not** creams). Skin tonic or witch-hazel-and-water also help. Skins that feel tight and dry need moisturisers.

Make-up is **good** for your skin, protecting it from very cold, very hot or very dry weather; it is bad **only** if you do not cleanse thoroughly.

Your nails Take as much care of your toe nails as your finger nails. If your nails break or crack, or if they have been weakened by biting, try eating 3 or 4 squares of jelly (straight from the packet) each day. In a month you will have beautiful nails.

Personal Freshness

Do wash tights and briefs **every** day.

Do wash all other underwear at least once a week.

Do check that dresses and sweaters have no stale smell.

It was written of Elizabeth I, "The Queen taketh a bath once a month, whether she need it or no." **We** need baths every day if we can get them; if not, wash under arms, between legs, and feet, **every** day.

Use a deodorant/anti-perspirant if you need one, but washing is still the best freshener. Be specially careful when you have a monthly period—do **not** stop having baths—if you are able to, use tampons (Tampax, Lil-lets).

YOUR FIGURE

The quickest way to a better figure is stand tall—walk tall—sit tall at work—relax your shoulders and hold in your middle.

If you practise this it will soon become a good habit and give you a trim figure all your life. **And** you will be healthier.

Many girls are plumper than they want to be—this fat will disappear naturally, but if you are **much** overweight, here is a safe and sure diet, safe even while you are still growing.

Cut right out. Biscuits, cakes, puddings, rice, spaghctti, macaroni, tinned fruit, jam, sugar, sweets, chocolate and ice cream.

Eat less of Potatoes, bread.

Eat as much as you want of Fresh fruit, salads or cooked vegetables, cheese, milk, butter, margarine, eggs, fish, lean or fat meat, thin soups, tea, coffee. Do not cut down on the amount you drink.

Always keep yourself warm when you are slimming, or your will feel miserable. A cup of tea is comforting and filling—a square of cheese stops hunger. **Ask your doctor** if you want to go on a really strict diet.

A beautiful figure is worth the trouble!

THREADS, FIBRES AND FABRICS

THREADS

These are used to make fabrics in two main ways:

Weaving with straight threads,
making **woven fabrics**

Weft threads at right angles to the selvedge and Warp threads.

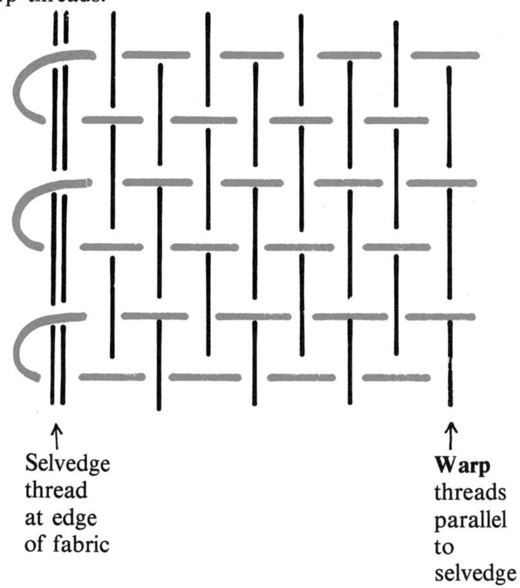

Knitting with looped threads, making **knit** or **jersey fabrics**

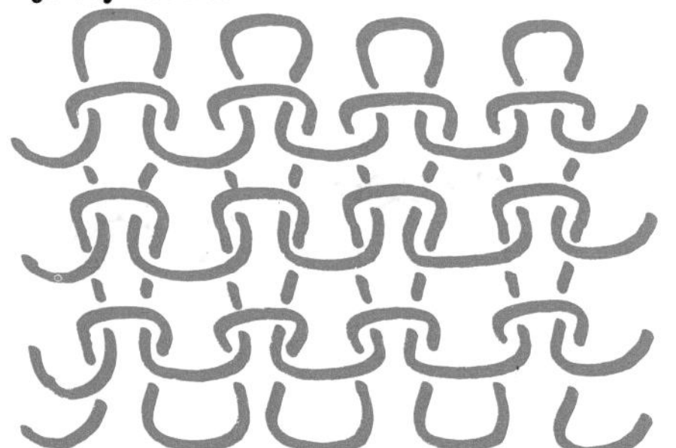

The **straight grain** of a fabric means the direction, parallel to the selvedge, where the cloth is least stretchy. Clothes hang better if the straight grain goes exactly up-and-down the garment.

Threads themselves are made from different animal or vegetable **fibres.** These fibres are in **short lengths** as you will see if you pull apart a piece of knitting wool. They are twisted together and pulled out into a thin, 1-ply thread—this is "spinning"—then two or more threads may be twisted together for greater strength, making 2, 3 or 4-ply threads.

In most **man-made** fibres, threads are made from hot liquid chemicals, squirted through small holes and cooled into long strips called **filaments.** These can be kept long for smooth fabrics; or cut into short lengths for spinning into thicker ones.

Some filaments are smooth, like Nylon

Some can be crimped, to give a springy, crease-resisting fabric, like Crimplene

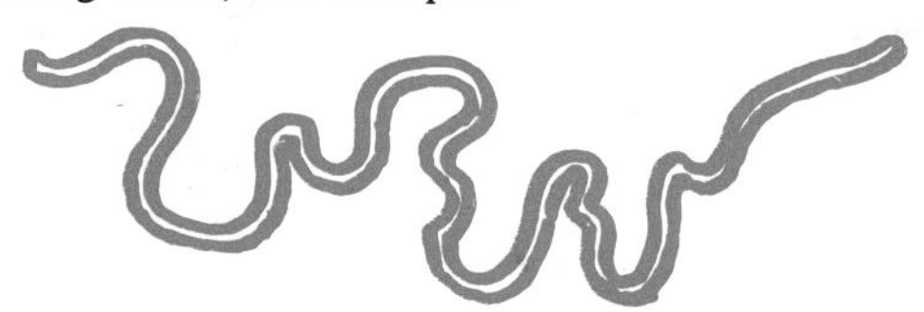

NATURAL FIBRES

Wool is the most important animal fibre, coming of course from the fleece of sheep. It is naturally springy, so it sheds creases easily, and naturally crinkly so that air trapped between the fibres makes it warm to wear. It is comfortable to wear because it absorbs dampness. As well as the thick or fluffy "woollen" fabrics, it can be made into smooth, strong, closely-woven men's suit fabrics, known as "worsteds".

Other animal fibres, all more expensive, can be treated like a wool:

Mohair—From the Angora Goat.
Angora—From the Angora Rabbit.
Cashmere—From the Cashmere Goat.
Camel, Vicuna and Llama—From those animals; but scarce and expensive.

Silk is made from single long threads unwound from the cocoon of the silk-worm, a caterpillar which feeds on mulberry leaves. It is a very thin, strong thread and is woven into the finest, softest fabrics, which drape well and have a beautiful soft sheen. Silk is very scarce and expensive, but *spun silk*, made from short, broken lengths of the fibre, is cheaper.

Cotton is made from the white fluffy fibres round the seeds of the cotton plant. The fibres can either be made into "cotton wool" or combed out and spun into cotton threads. Cotton is cheap (but becoming dearer), strong, easily washed and cool to wear; it absorbs damp so is comfortable in hot weather. It creases easily unless treated with special finishes.

Linen comes from the stringy stalks of the flax plant. It has the same good points as cotton, but is stronger, smoother and much more expensive. Linen thread is used for buttonholes and sewing on buttons.

MAN-MADE FIBRES

Man-made fibres (which used to be called **synthetics**), are made either from cellulose or from chemicals found in oil, coal, etc. They are all liquids at some stage of manufacture. They have many uses because:

1. Their raw materials are cheap and plentiful, so the fabrics can be cheap.
2. They are easy to wash, do not shrink or stretch, and need little or no ironing.
3. They dry very quickly, so that underwear can be washed and worn again the next day.
4. They are mothproof and many are flame-resistant.

These are the most useful man-made fibres:

Viscose rayon (Sarille, Vincel, Evlan)—This is a soft, fluffy, warm fibre, made from the cellulose in wood-pulp. Very widely used because it is cheap and washes well. Rayon is strong when dry, but weak when wet, so it must be ironed dry. Sarille is used for dress fabrics which look like fine wool. Vincel is often mixed with cotton for underwear, and Evlan is used for carpets. The new Darelle is flame-resistant.

Acetate (Dicel, Lansil) and Tri-acetate (Tricel) —These are made from cellulose found in wood-pulp or cotton lint. They are smooth, shiny fabrics, making good "silky" dress fabrics and slippery coat linings. They are cheap and strong. Lo-Flam Dicel is flame-resistant.

Nylon (The name for these fibres is **poly-amide**, and it includes Bri-Nylon, Celon, Banlon and Enkalon). Extremely strong, and usually made as a filament, from chemicals including benzine and from oil. It stretches and springs back well, and needs little ironing, so it is useful for underwear, tights and easy-care dress fabrics. Woven nylon can feel hot and clammy in warm weather, as it does not absorb dampness. Nylon is also used for ropes, and Enkalon is the kind of Nylon used for carpets.

Polyesters (Terylene, Dacron, Crimplene, Lirelle, Trevira, Terlenka)—These are made from petroleum chemicals, including the "anti-freeze" used in car radiators. They are hard fibres, making a firm cloth, either woven or knitted. They are often mixed with wool, rayon or cotton, especially for pleated skirts.

Acrylics (Acrilan, Courtelle, Orlon, Dralon, Dynel and the flame-proof Teklan). These are softer fibres, more like wool, and mostly used for knitwear or jersey materials. They attract dirt, so pale colours should be washed often and stored in polythene bags. Dynel is used for wigs and fake fur.

Elastic fibres (Lycra, Spanzelle)—These are mainly used for bras, girdles and swim wear, because they stretch and spring back well, and are easily washed. Do not iron.

FABRICS

1. Dictionary of woven fabrics

Do not try to learn all these—You can look them up here when you need them.

Bouclé A rough and knobbly surface, made by looped threads, usually in wool for coats.

Brocade A patterned weave, using several colours or metal threads, for dress or furnishing materials; in cotton, silk, rayon, acetate or Tricel.

Calico Cheap, strong, rough-surfaced cotton fabric for aprons, etc.

Canvas Heavy, close-woven cotton for dungarees, coats, etc.

Chiffon Sheer, soft silk, nylon or rayon fabric for blouses or scarves.

Ciré A shiny, wet-look weave in acetate or Tricel.

Cloqué Woven with a blistered surface, made by some warp threads being pulled up tighter—a dress fabric in cotton or rayon.

Corduroy Firm weave with a velvety rib and one-way nap. Made of cotton and used for trousers, pinafore dresses, etc.

Crêpe Dull-surfaced, slightly stretchy fabric in rayon, cotton, wool or silk, for soft dresses or blouses. It drapes well, hanging in soft folds.

Damask A pattern made by dull and shiny threads, for dress and household fabrics, in cotton, rayon or linen.

Denim Firm, strong fabric with diagonal weave and weft threads in a lighter colour. Used for overalls, jeans, skirts. Usually cotton, but stretch-denim also contains nylon.

Faille Fine "silky" weave, with slight weft-wise rib, usually in silk, rayon, Tricel.

Flannel Medium-thick wool with a soft surface, used for skirts, trousers.

Fur fabric Long-pile fabric, used for coats; of rayon, wool or man-made fibres on a cotton backing.

Gabardine Tightly woven with a strong diagonal rib, in wool, cotton or rayon for coats, trousers or skirts.

Georgette Sheer, but thicker than chiffon. Dull surface. Used for blouses and dresses in silk, rayon or Tricel.

Gingham Plain, firm weave in striped or checked cotton, for children's wear or summer dresses.

Hopsack A weaving pattern using threads in pairs each way. In wool, linen or blends for skirts or dresses.

Jacquard Woven (or knitted) patterns in several colours, giving a "tapestry" or many-coloured design. Usually in wool, cotton or polyester.

Lawn Thin, light-weight weave of cotton or polyester, for blouses or nightwear.

Muslin Semi-sheer cotton with soft or crisp finish, mainly used as interfacing.

Nap Fabrics that have **nap** are ones that feel smooth if stroked in one direction and rough if stroked the other way.

Needlecord A cotton weave like corduroy, but with a finer rib.

Organdie Sheer, very crisp, dull-surfaced cotton for blouses or interfacing.

Organza Sheer, crisp and shiny fabric in silk, nylon or Tricel for blouses.

Ottoman Very stiff weave, with a thick rib, in wool, silk, rayon or Tricel for coats or evening wear.

Panne velvet Velvet with a flattened nap and strong one-way shine, in rayon, nylon or cotton, for trousers, evening wear. Stretch-velvet includes nylon.

Percale Dull-surfaced firm weave in cotton. The ordinary "dress cottons".

Pile Cut threads standing up from the fabric, as in velvet or fake fur.

Piqué Raised rib or dot, with a shiny finish, in cotton, rayon or Tricel for dresses, blouses, collars, cuffs.

Plissé Woven with plain and puckered stripes, a cotton for blouses.

Plush Long-pile "silky" weave, deeper than velvet, in rayon or silk.

Poplin Plain, firmly-woven cotton with a slight rib, for shirts and blouses.

Repp Firm weave with weft-wise rib, but thinner than Ottoman. Cotton or wool.

Sailcloth Firm, close-woven cotton, lighter in weight than canvas, for coats, dresses.

Sateen Shiny weave in cotton or rayon, showing mostly the weft threads. Used for linings and cheap dresses.

Satin Shiny weave in silk, Tricel or acetate showing mostly the warp threads. Can be thin for blouses, or thick and stiff for evening wear, wedding dresses.

Seersucker Puckered stripes or checks, made by some threads being more tightly woven. Used for cotton or nylon blouses, dresses, household fabrics.

Serge Diagonal weave with a flat surface, in wool, for coats or suits.

Slub A ridged surface made by uneven thickness or lumps in the weft threads. Silk, linen or man-made fibres.

Surah Close, twilled weave of silk, Tricel or acetate for ties, blouses.

Taffeta Plain, crisp, shiny weave in rayon, Tricel, nylon or silk, for dresses, linings.

Terry cloth Towelling weave, looped on one or both sides, for dresses, bath-robes, towels, curtains. Cotton; but stretch terry cloth also contains nylon.

Tweed Rough-surfaced, coarse-woven wool, often checked, for coats, suits.

Twill A weaving pattern making diagonal lines or ribs. Can be used with any thickness of thread and any fibre. Gabardine, denim, serge and surah are all twilled weaves.

Velvet Close pile weave giving a rich, deep effect, in silk, rayon or nylon.

Velveteen Close, short pile in cotton, for dresses or suède-like jackets.

Voile Open-weave sheer cotton or polyester with dull finish, for blouses, shirts.

Worsted A tightly-twisted kind of smooth woollen thread, making fine, closely-woven cloths, mostly for men's suits. Keeps its shape better than other woollens, but is more expensive.

2. Jersey Jersey has many good points; stretch where it is wanted, making a more comfortable fit—freedom from fraying, so edge-neatening is simpler—warmth with lightness because so much air is trapped in the knitting. Jersey is sometimes knitted in the shape of a tube, then flattened and slit along one edge. The fold at the other side may not press out, so do not use this fold when cutting out.

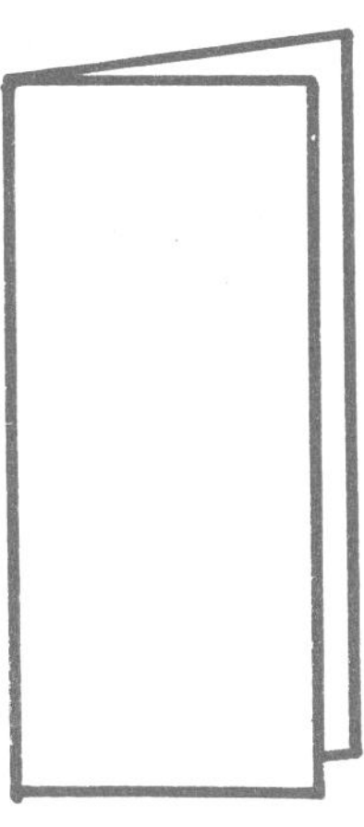

Any fibres may be used in jerseys—wool, cotton, rayons, nylon, Tricel; but polyesters and acrylics are much more often seen as jerseys than as woven fabrics.

Single jersey (Stockinette) is thin, stretches both ways, and is knitted on one row of needles. It looks like fine hand knitting, and can be used for stockings and tights. In wool, it can be used for dresses. It is difficult to handle, because it easily stretches out of shape.

Double jersey This is firmer, and is knitted on two rows of needles. Courtelle, Crimplene or wool double jerseys are used for suits or dresses. It is easy to handle and keeps its shape very well. Right and wrong sides both look alike.

Warp-knit jersey is knitted in rows along the length, or warp, of the fabric. It stretches weft-wise but not warp-wise, so is useful for trousers and skirts. Nylon warp-knit is used for shirts and the thinner nylon tricot for underwear.

Raschel-knit A new method of knitting, which always shows a slight zig-zag stitch. It is specially useful for lacy patterns, but can be used with any thickness of thread. Its best point is that it stretches, slightly, but always returns **exactly** to its shape.

3. Bonded fabrics These are neither woven nor knitted, but their fibres are tangled and pressed together in a thick layer. We shall see many more bonded fabrics in future, making "paper" dresses, curtains, scouring cloths, etc.

Felt is bonded, made from wool fibre. Used for hats, skirts, furnishings.

Vilene is also bonded; it is a man-made fibre used for interfacing.

4. Foambacked fabrics (These also may be called **bonded**, in shops.) They are made by sticking 2 or 3 layers of fabric together in a "sandwich". The right side may be woven or knitted or the leather-like Vinyl. The wrong side is usually a thin acetate jersey. The middle of the sandwich may be a thin layer of plastic foam. Foam backing keeps the material to its original shape, helps it to shed creases, and gives it strength and warmth. It also saves having to line the garment. But it is expensive to manufacture, and if the layers are stuck together unevenly, or off the straight grain, nothing can be done to put them right.

5. Fabric finishes Fabrics can be given special chemical treatments during manufacture:

Water repellent finishes—Dri-Sil. Scotchgard.

Shrink-proofing—Sanforized.

Mothproofing—Dielmoth.

Minimum Iron—Tebilized. Belofast.

Flame resistant—Proban. Timonox. (Use soapless detergents only and do not soak or bleach.)

These finishes may be spoiled if the garments are wrongly washed or ironed, so be very careful to follow the maker's instructions exactly.

6. Dyeing and printing Fibres can be dyed to their final colour before weaving. This is **yarn-dyeing.** In man-made fibres, the liquid chemical can be dyed even before it becomes a fibre, and it will never fade. Plain coloured fabrics can be made in this way; or by using threads of different colours fabrics can be checked, striped or tapestry-patterned.

Some plain-coloured fabrics are **piece-dyed** after being woven; they may not be as colour-fast as yarn-dyed fabrics.

For printed patterns, the cloth must first be woven or knitted, and then passed round printing rollers which carry the dye colours, and press them on to the fabric. This is why printed fabrics show stronger colouring on the right side.

3 YOUR SEWING EQUIPMENT

YOUR WORK-BOX, which could be a large biscuit tin, should have in it:

Dress-making shears with long blades for smooth cutting. They must be used **only** for cutting out dress fabrics—cutting paper blunts them.

Small, sharp-pointed scissors, for snipping, trimming and general use. Keep your scissors dry and clean and they will stay sharp longer.

Pins A box of fine steel "dressmakers" pins. Leave the black paper in the box as it helps to keep pins free from rust. Always throw away bent, rusty or blunt pins.

Needles Have plenty of different kinds and sizes.
"Sharps" have egg-shaped eyes and are for hand-sewing on dress fabrics.

"Crewel" needles have long eyes for thicker embroidery threads; also useful if you are bad at threading small eyes.

Needle sizes are from 1 (very thick) to 10 (very fine).

No. 7 is a useful middling size for dressmaking.

Thimble, to fit the middle finger of the hand in which you hold your needle. Using it to push your needle through the fabric will help you to sew faster and with less trouble, so it is worth making an effort to get used to a thimble.

Tape measure This should be 5′ 0″ (or 1·5 metres) long, and made of strong plastic or fibreglass, so that it will not stretch. It is useful to have inches on one side and centimetres on the other.

Threads You will need sewing threads for machining and hand sewing, to match your fabric. If you cannot get an exact match, choose a colour a little darker or duller—it will show up less.

Coats' Satinised or **Dewhurst's Sylko** are shiny cotton threads to use with all fabrics except man-made; they are most useful in No. 40 thickness, but you can also buy the finer No. 50.

Coats' Drima or **Dewhurst's Trylko** or **Gütermann Mara** are polyester threads for use on **any** fabrics; they are in one thickness only.

You will also need **tacking threads**, which are best in white or a different colour from your fabric, so that they show up. Special cotton thread, made for tacking, is cheap, soft, and does not slip out of place easily; or you can use up the ends of old reels of sewing thread—never waste oddments. **Button threads** are thicker, stronger, and usually made of linen. Use them also for sewing on skirt hooks and for making hand-worked buttonholes. **Gütermann Hela** is a good silky buttonhole twist.

LARGER PIECES OF EQUIPMENT YOU WILL NEED

Sewing table for laying out patterns and cutting out your material. If you have no table large enough, cut out on a carpeted floor.

Full length mirror, to check that your garment is hanging straight, hem level.

Electric iron Your iron should have 4 heat settings for different fabrics (page 12). A steam iron is useful, but not essential, for all fabrics which are usually ironed damp. (Switch off the steam for dry ironing.)

Use distilled water if your tap water is hard.

Empty the iron after use so that it does not "fur up" like a kettle.

The **sole plate** of your iron must always be kept clean and shiny—to clean, rub it gently, when cold, with a damp scouring pad, such as "Brillo", or with "Ironcleen", and make sure that all traces of soap are wiped away with a clean, damp cloth. Mind that no water runs over the sides or top of the iron.

For safety, **never** do your ironing while standing on a damp concrete floor: a faulty iron could give you a bad electric shock.

Ironing board Should be adjustable to a comfortable height for you. It should be well padded and have a cover that slips off for washing.

A narrow **sleeve-board** is also useful for slipping into a sleeve to press a single thickness. **A tailor's pad** (a small hard cushion) can be used under the curved parts of garments, such as the shoulders, so that the iron does not flatten them. An **ironing cloth** of thin cotton is needed for damp pressing.

SEWING MACHINE

This is the most important dressmaking aid of all. With it, you can sew more quickly, more evenly and more strongly than by hand.

With a straight-stitching hand machine, by using different attachments or by turning a dial, you can also:
- Make a narrow hem
- Put on bias binding
- Stitch in a zip
- Make gathers.

A straight-stitching electric machine does all this and leaves both your hands free to guide your work.

A swing-needle electric machine will also do:
- Buttonholes
- Sewing on of buttons
- Stretch seams on jersey fabrics
- Edge-neatening by zig-zag stitching
- Darning
- Satin stitch.

Threading the machine Learn the maker's threading chart. The top thread and the bobbin thread must both be placed exactly as the diagrams show, so that both threads end up equally tight. This is most important in making a firm stitch. **Always try the stitch first on a spare scrap of your fabric, folded double.** Check these points:

1. Are the top and bottom threads equally tight? The stitch should look like this (side view).

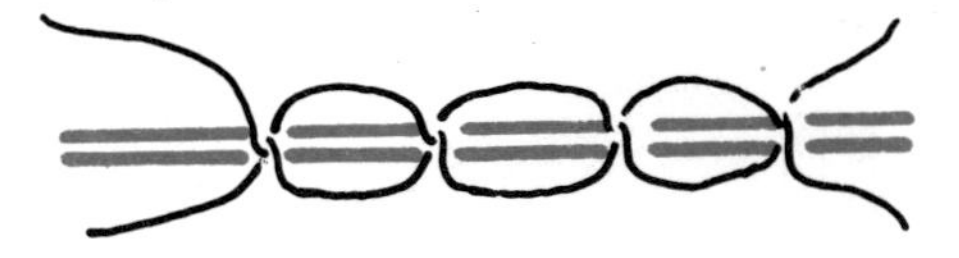

If it looks like this, the top thread is too loose. Tighten the screw or dial that controls it.

If it looks like this, the top thread is too tight. Loosen the screw or dial.

Do not try to alter the tightness of the bottom thread.

2. Is the stitch the right length?
   12 stitches to the inch for thin fabrics and jerseys.
   10 stitches to the inch for thick fabrics.
   6–7 stitches to the inch for gathering or machine-basting.

3. Is the machine needle the right size?
   Size 80 for thin fabrics.
   Size 90 for general use.
   Size 100 for heavy fabrics.

4. Is the needle screwed in tightly, the right way round? Is the presser foot on firmly?

How to keep your machine in good order

1. See that the needle is sharp and straight—or it may break or miss stitches.
2. Never run the machine threaded but without material—the threads will tangle.
3. Never let anyone else turn the handle for you, or press the foot control—that way **you** lose control.
4. Brush out any fluff from round the bobbin or teeth, under the needle.
5. Keep the machine covered and dust-free when not in use.
6. Put **one** drop of machine oil in each oil-hole once a month—more often if you use the machine regularly.

YOUR PATTERN

CHOOSING A PATTERN

Choose your material first.
Then buy a pattern to suit it.
Then buy the right length of material.

Make sure the pattern suits the material—
Pleats need a firm weave. Gathers need a soft, thin fabric. Close-fitting trousers need a strong fabric, or a stretchy jersey.

Is it a good make of pattern? Has it an Instruction Sheet that shows each step clearly? Very cheap patterns, or ones from magazines, may have poor instructions that are difficult to follow. A good pattern is worth its cost. With care, it can be used many times over. "Simplicity", "Style", "Butterick's" and "McCall's" are all good, fashionable, middle-priced patterns.

Is the pattern easy enough for you? Begin with the easiest styles, such as plain skirts, trousers, shorts, plain dresses without sleeves. Then go on to dresses or blouses with sleeves, gathers or collars, Jackets and dresses with pleats or curved seams are more difficult to do well. When you can work easily with thin, firm fabrics, try the thicker woollens and knits.

TAKING YOUR MEASUREMENTS

There are 4 important measurements:

Bust. Keep the tape measure high at the back, and take it across the widest part of the bust in front.

Waist. Comfortably tight, as you would have a skirt waistband.

Hips. Measure round the widest part of the hip, 7″–9″ (18–23 cm) below the waist.

Back waist length. From the bone you can feel at the back of your neck just below the collar, take the measurement down to your waist. This makes sure that the dress waistline will match yours.

Choose patterns by these body measurements —the patterns themselves are about 2″ (5 cms) bigger at bust and hip to allow for an easy fit when walking or sitting.

FINDING YOUR PATTERN SIZE

There are different sets of patterns for different figure types. Here are some of them, the same in all makes of pattern. There is usually a 2″ (5 cm) difference between one size and the next.

Misses Patterns are for girls with developed figures, who are 5′ 5″–5′ 6″ tall (165–168 cm). The bust is 2″ (5 cm) smaller than the hip. Here are a few **misses** sizes:

Size No.	*10*
Bust	32½″ (83 cm)
Waist	24″ (61 cm)
Hip, 9″ (23 cm) below waist	34½″ (88 cm)
Back Waist Length	16″ (40·5 cm)
Size No.	*12*
Bust	34″ (87 cm)
Waist	25·5″ (65 cm)
Hip, 9″ (23 cm) below waist	36″ (91 cm)
Back Waist Length	16¼″ (41·5 cm)
Size No.	*14*
Bust	36″ (92 cm)
Waist	27″ (69 cm)
Hip, 9″ (23 cm) below waist	38″ (97 cm)
Back Waist Length	16½″ (42 cm)

Young Junior/Teen Patterns are for growing teenage girls about 5′ 1″–5′ 3″ (155–160 cm), whose bust is still developing. The bust is 3″ (7 cm) smaller than the hips.

Size No.	*9/10*
Bust	30½″ (78 cm)
Waist	24″ (61 cm)
Hip, 7″ (18 cm) below waist	33½″ 85 cm)
Back Waist Length	14½″ (37 cm)
Size No.	*11/12*
Bust	32″ (82 cm)
Waist	25″ (63 cm)
Hip, 7″ (18 cm) below waist	35″ (89 cm)
Back Waist Length	15″ (38 cm)
Size No.	*13/14*
Bust	33½″ (86 cm)
Waist	26″ (66 cm)
Hip, 7″ (18 cm) below waist	36½″ (93 cm)
Back Waist Length	15¾″ (39 cm)

Junior Petite Patterns are for shorter girls about 5′ 0″–5′ 1″ (153–155 cm) whose bust is already developed. The bust is only 1″ (2 cm) smaller than the hips, and there is only a 1″ difference between sizes.

Size No.	*9JP*
Bust	33″ (84 cm)
Waist	24½″ (62 cm)
Hip, 7″ (18 cm) below waist	34″ (86 cm)
Back Waist Length	14¾″ (37·5 cm)
Size No.	*11JP*
Bust	34″ (87 cm)
Waist	25½″ (65 cm)
Hip, 7″ (18 cm)	35″ (89 cm)
Back Waist Length below waist	15¼″ (38·5 cm)
Size No.	*13JP*
Bust	35″ (89 cm)
Waist	26½″ (67 cm)
Hip, 7″ (18 cm) below waist	36″ (91 cm)
Back Waist Length	15″ (38 cm)

Do not try to learn all these sizes. Just learn **your own size.** But remember that you grow.

If no size of pattern matches **all** your measurements, buy the size that **suits your height and fits your bust.** It is easier to alter patterns at the hip and waist—not so easy to alter necklines, collars or shoulders.

Do not make large alterations—about 2″ (5 cm) is the most you should alter. The following are easy alterations:

For a larger waist

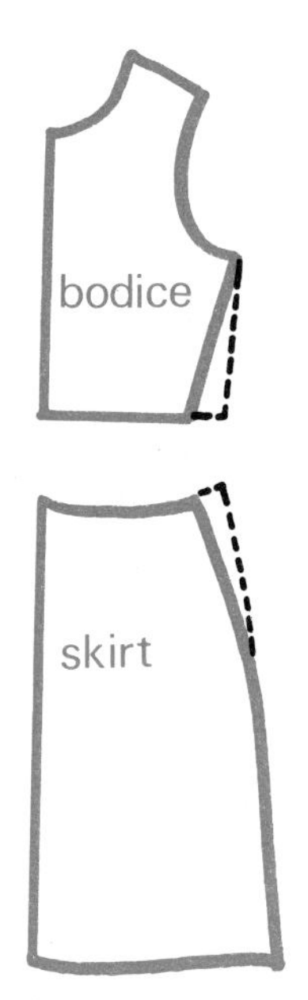

Add a quarter of the extra measurement needed, to each side-back and side-front edge.
$\frac{1}{2}$″ (1 cm) extra on each edge, front and back, will give a total of 2″ extra on the whole garment.

For a smaller waist

Make darts at the waistline of bodice and skirt.

Fold pattern and pin.

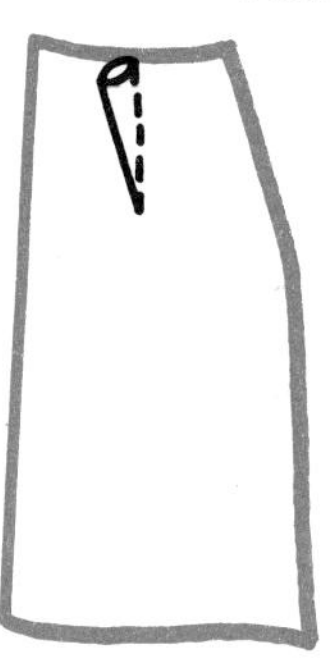

For larger hips. Make the pattern wider by cutting it, spreading the pieces apart, and pinning them to a strip of paper. If this makes the waist too large, make darts at the waist after the fabric has been cut out.

For a skirt, add half of the extra measurement to the front, half to the back.

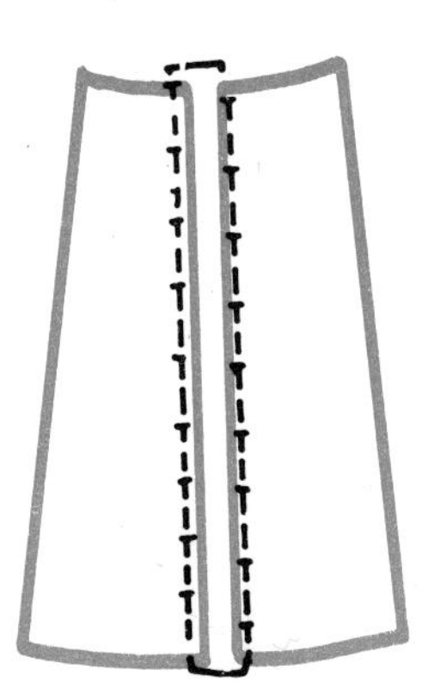

For trousers or shorts, add a quarter of the extra needed to the fronts, and a quarter to the backs.

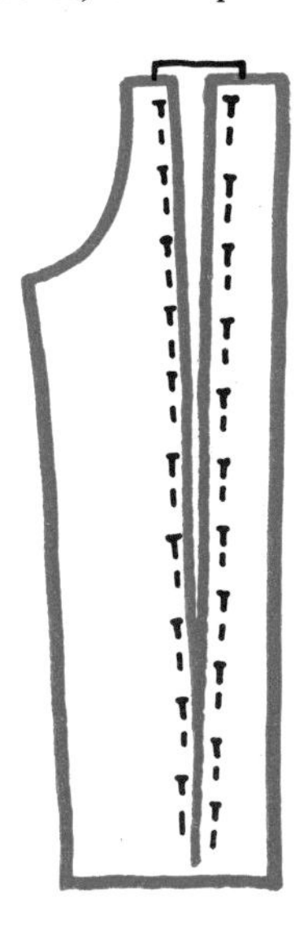

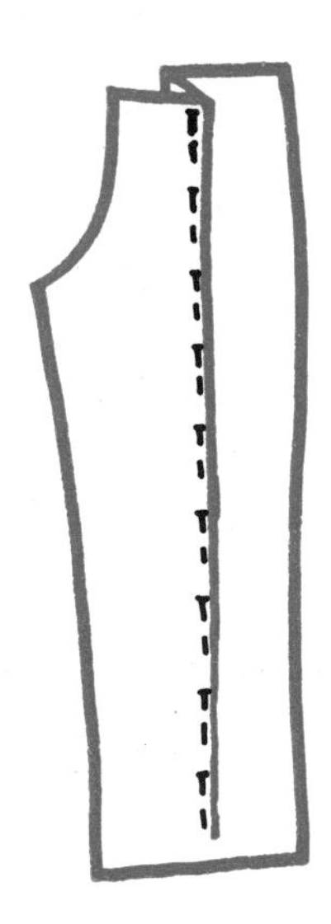

For trousers, the pleat on the front leg and the pleat on the back leg should each take a quarter of the total. Taper the pleat to nothing.

For smaller hips. Make a pleat in the pattern, front and back, remembering that each pleat will take up twice its own width:

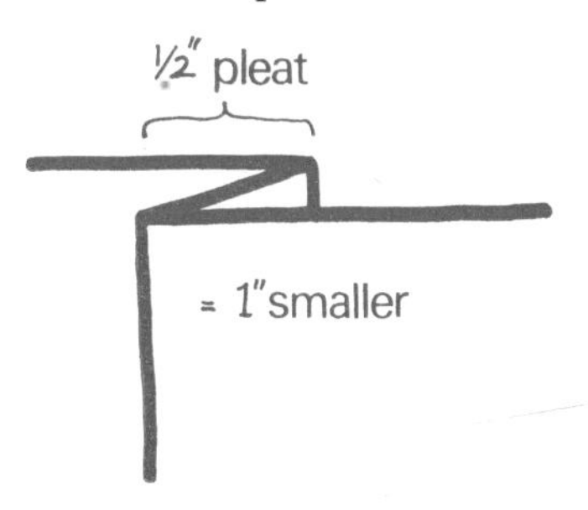

For a skirt, pleat equally at back and front.

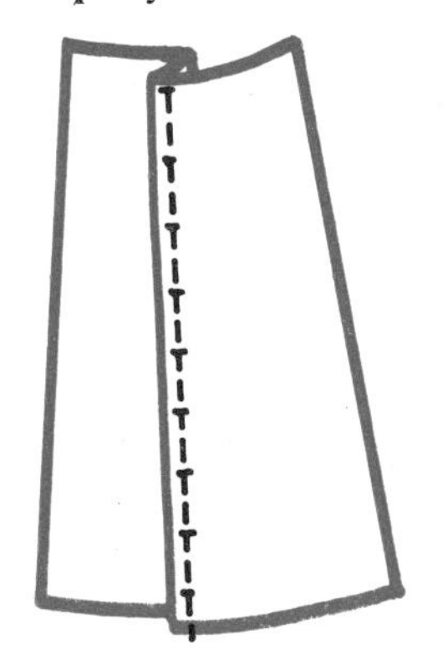

To lengthen patterns. Cut and spread the pattern pieces apart to give the extra length needed. For *straight* skirts or sleeves, do not cut the pattern, but add length at the lower edge.

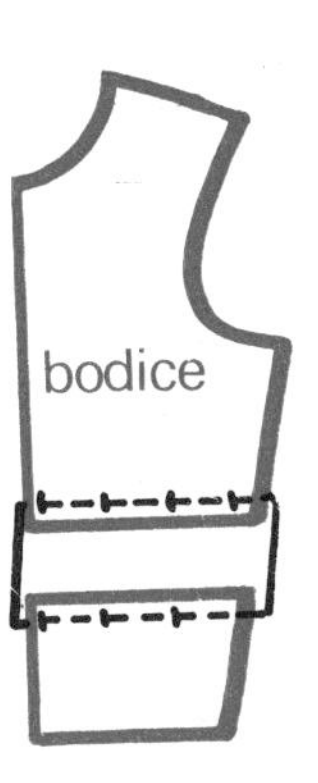

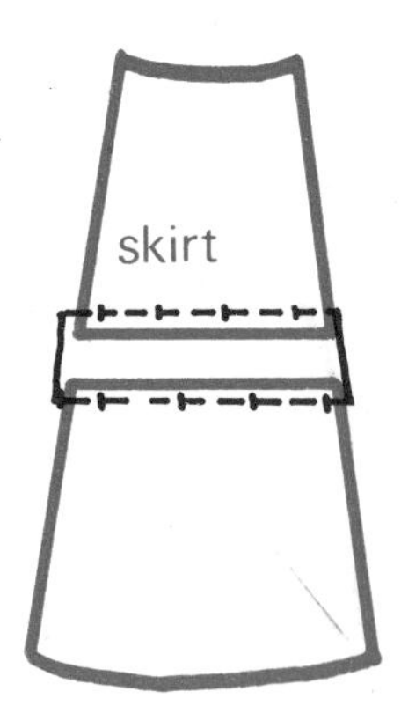

Note: cut through bodice pattern *below* any underarm dart.

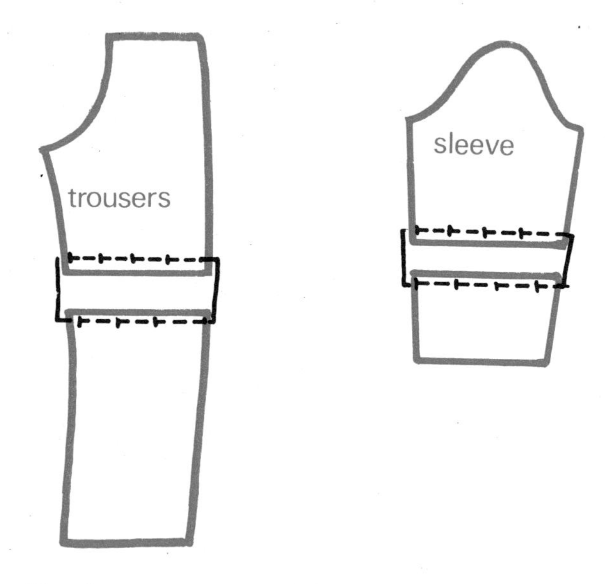

To shorten patterns. Pleat the pattern. Each pleat will take up twice its own measurement.

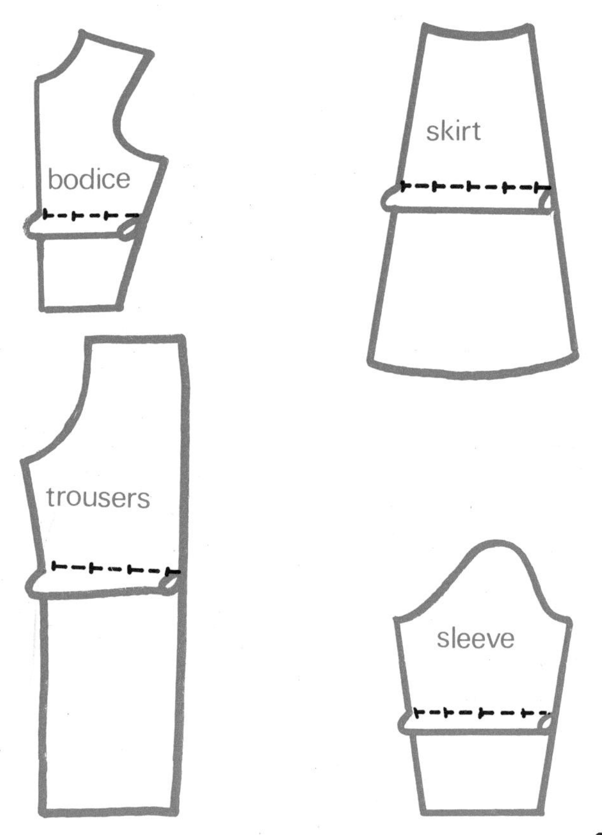

RECKONING THE MATERIAL NEEDED

Your Pattern Envelope will show you how much material you need for your size, width of fabric and choice of style.

Most thin fabrics are 36″ (92 cm) wide.
Some man-made materials are 45″ (114 cm) wide.
Most thick or woollen fabrics are 54″ (137 cm) wide.
But jerseys may be 60″ (152 cm) wide, or more.

If you **must** buy fabric before choosing your pattern, this is the amount you would need:

For a straight or A-Line sleeveless dress or blouse in 36″ fabric. Twice the finished length from the shoulder. The hems and turnings make up for the overlap of the pattern pieces, if laid out like this:

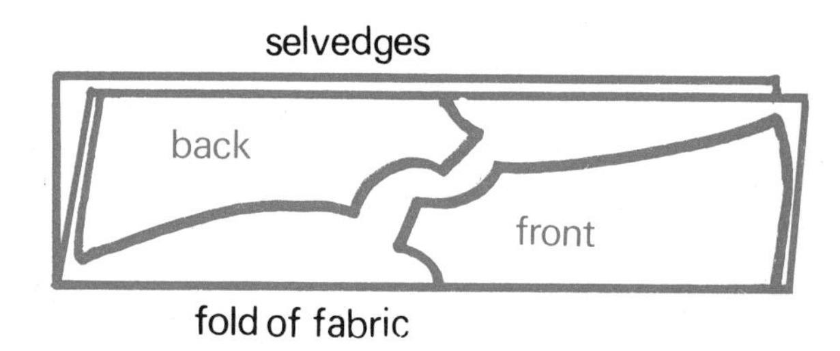

This layout works for a plain fabric, but more material would be needed for fabric with nap or a one-way design.

A plain dress in 54″ (137 cm) material. Will need the finished length plus 6″ (15 cm).

Long sleeves in 36″ material will need $\frac{3}{4}$ yard (69 cm). Each sleeve takes half the width.

Short sleeves in 36″ material will need $\frac{3}{8}$–$\frac{1}{2}$ yard (34–46 cm)

A skirt in 36″ material will need twice the finished length. (In sizes smaller than 32″ (81 cm) hip, a straight skirt can be made from only once the finished length plus 6″, as back and front can be cut from half the width each.)

A skirt in 54″ material will need the finished length plus 6″.

Trousers in 36″ material will need twice the finished length.

Trousers in 54″ material will need the finished length plus 6″.

Up to a quarter of a yard (23 cm) extra may be needed to match large checks or patterns.

THE COST OF YOUR GARMENT will be:

The price per yard of fabric, multiplied by the number of yards. Also lining, if any.

The price of the pattern—but you may use this again.

The price of thread, zip, buttons, etc. (called "Sewing Notions" on your pattern envelope).

Work out the cost of different garments, and see how much cheaper they are to make than to buy. (Some garments, for instance slips and briefs, may be cheaper to buy; also the fabrics they are made from cannot always be bought by the yard.)

PATTERN MARKINGS, printed on the pattern pieces, are these;

Straight grain mark. Place the arrow so that both ends are the same distance away from the selvedge of the fabric. This makes sure that the warp threads go exactly up and down the garment, so that it will hang straight when you wear it.

Fold marking. Place the points of the bent arrow **right on** a fold of the fabric. The fold should be along a warp thread, and may be the centre front line or the centre back line of your garment.

Cutting line

Fitting, or stitching, line.

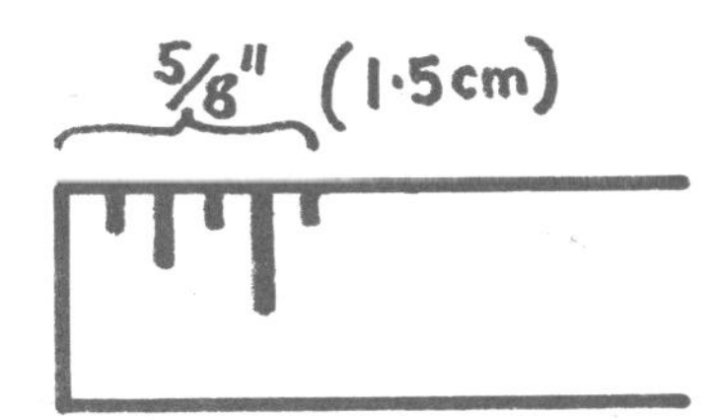

Seam allowance. This is the distance between the cutting and stitching lines, almost always $\frac{5}{8}$″ (1·5 cm).

Lengthening or shortening line.

Balance marks, or notches, to match when seaming two pieces of the garment together.

PREPARING TO CUT OUT

1. Press out any deep creases in your fabric.
2. Straighten the ends by pulling a thread, or cutting along the line of a thread, from selvedge to selvedge. If the corners are not square, try pulling them. Some fabrics with a permanent finish will not square up.

3. See if there is any one-way pattern or "feel" to the fabric. This is a **nap**, and when there is one, all pattern pieces must be cut out with their tops pointing the same way. Use the pattern's "With Nap" layout.
4. Find the *Instruction Sheet* in your pattern, and pick the right **layout** for your size, width of fabric, choice of style and nap, if any.
5. Put back in the envelope any pattern pieces you are not using.
6. Fold your fabric right side inside (or, if a single thickness, right side up), as shown on the layout. Most often, fabric is folded along its length, with the selvedges pinned together. Smooth the fabric out on a large table, or on a carpeted floor if your table is not big enough.
7. Place all the pattern pieces, printed side **up**, on the fabric as shown in the layout. The printed cutting lines must not overlap each other. If the layout shows a shaded piece, this must be laid with the printed side **down**.

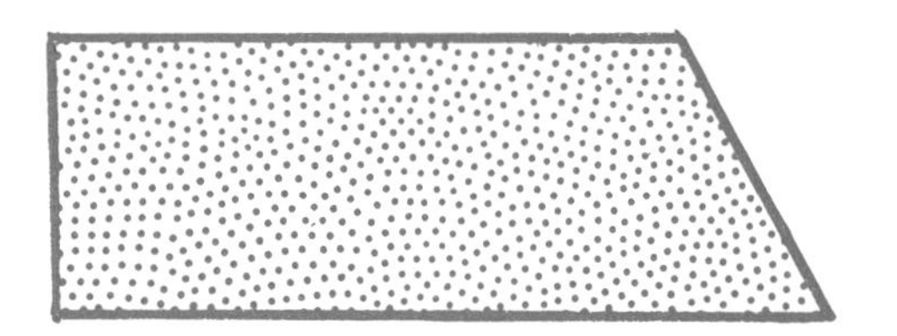

8. Pin all the pieces to the fabric along the **stitching line**, with pins at each corner and every 3″–6″ (8–15 cm) between. Do **not** pin on or outside the cutting line. Fabric and pattern must lie quite flat, without wrinkles.
9. Cut out with large cutting-out shears, and keep the lower blade (the round-ended one) touching the table. Never cut out holding your fabric up in the air. Cut **exactly** along the cutting lines, making sharp corners round the outside of notches. Leave the pattern pieces pinned in place.

MARKING YOUR FABRIC

You will need to transfer onto your fabric some pattern markings such as:

Darts	Pleats	Gathers
Buttonholes	Pockets	Seam Allowances

There are three ways of doing this:

1. Tailor's tacks. With double thread of a different colour from your fabric, make a tiny stitch through the dot or mark. Leave a loop of thread $\frac{1}{2}''$ (or 1·5 cm) long, and make another tiny stitch on top of the first. You now have two stitches going through the pattern and both layers of fabric.

Seen from above

Now lift the pattern off carefully, tearing it as little as possible, and then separate the layers of fabric gently and snip the threads between them. Both layers are now marked with thread.

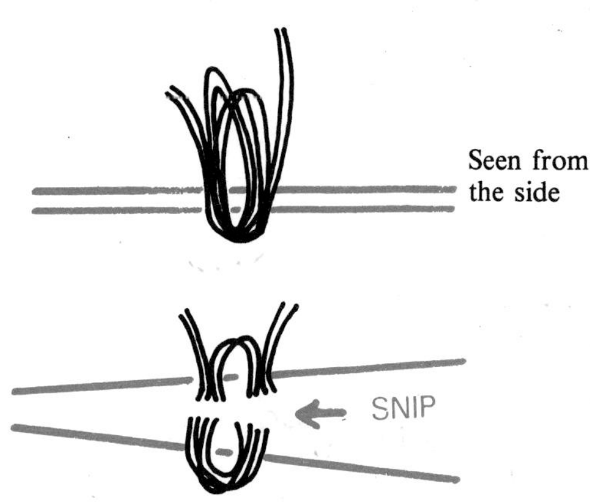

If your fabric is light coloured, do not use, e.g., a strong red for your tacks as this can sometimes leave a colour mark on your garment.

2. Carbon paper and tracing wheel Use Dressmaker's Carbon Paper in a different colour from your fabric. Slip the carbon under the pattern, folded so that the coloured side of the carbon is against the **wrong** sides of the fabric. Use the wheel heavily, making a cross at each mark, and both layers of fabric will then be marked. (With thick fabrics, mark each layer separately.)

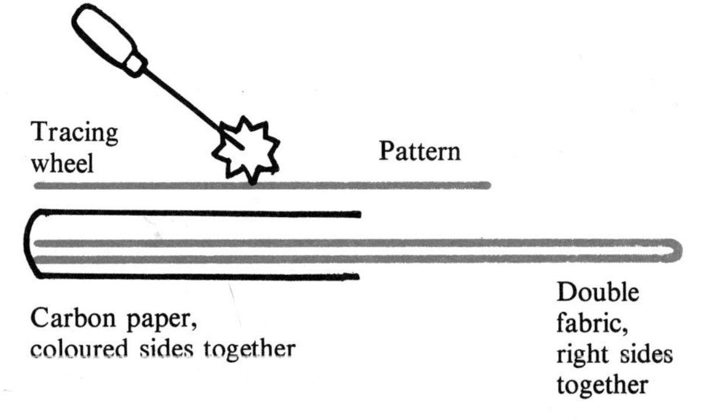

3. Dress-marker chalk. A flat piece of marking chalk is put under the fabric, and a chalk dress-marker pencil is used on top, pushed through the paper pattern. Both fabric layers are marked at once.

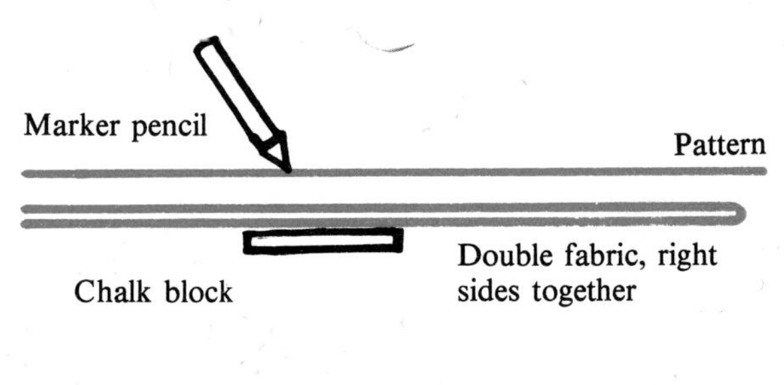

MAKING YOUR GARMENT

THE THREE MOST IMPORTANT STITCHES

Learn these three stitches perfectly, and you are half-way to being a dressmaker.

1. Tacking (also called **basting**). This is used to hold two pieces of fabric **firmly together** until you have tried on the garment and then machined or hand-sewn it.

   To start, take three small stitches at the same spot, and pull them up tightly.

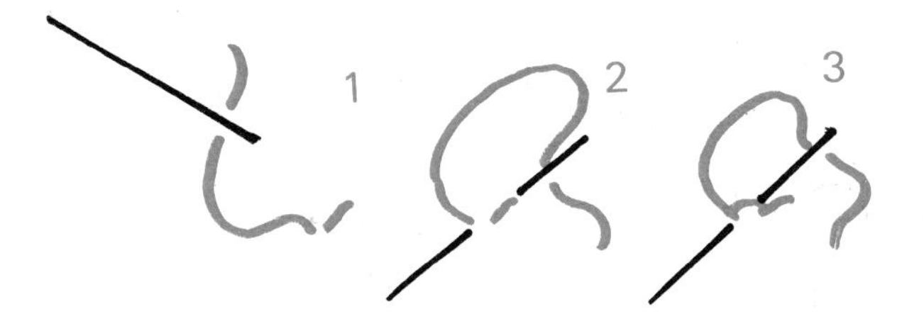

Then carry on with stitches ½″ (1 cm) long, or smaller for difficult places. The stitches may be placed evenly or in long and short pairs:

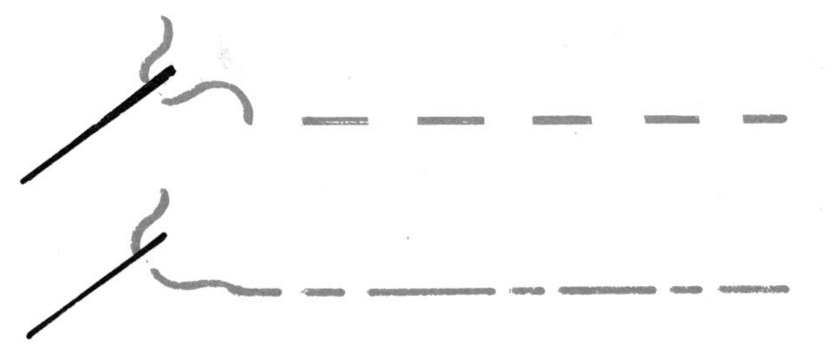

Finish off firmly with two stitches at the same spot. Basting can also mean another kind of tacking, which is useful for holding pleats in place, or setting in zip fasteners:

2. Running This is like tacking, but as small as you can make it. Start and finish off in same way. If you use a thimble, you can take up 3 or 4 stitches on the needle at once. Running is used for stitching seams.

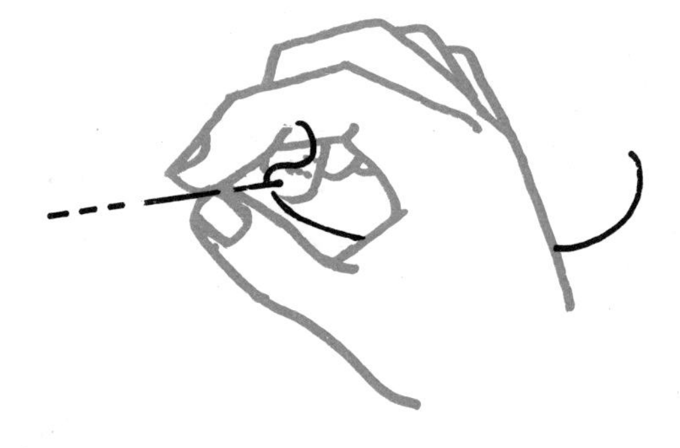

3. Back-stitching This is a very strong stitch —it does not come undone easily, even if a thread breaks. Begin and finish off like running. The stitch goes **back** a short way

on top, and **forward** a longer way underneath:

The sideways view is like this:

SHAPING THE PIECES

One of the main problems in dressmaking is that fabric is flat and people are round. So the pieces of a garment have to be **shaped** before they are seamed together. This is sometimes called "Control of Fullness". There are four ways to do it.

1. Darts Little folds of fabric, wider at the edge and narrowing to a point. They help to give a smooth fit at the shoulder, bust, waist, hip.

   Fold the fabric with right side inside. Pin the dart through each pair of marks, keeping in a straight line. The single mark is the end of the dart. Tack through the marks to the point. Stitch from the wide end to the point by machine. At the very point, leave the needle down in the work, raise the presser foot of the machine, swing the work round on the needle, and go back 6 stitches **over** the ones just done. This finishes the dart—or any machining—quite safely. (If you reverse the machine, instead, it is difficult to see where you are going.)

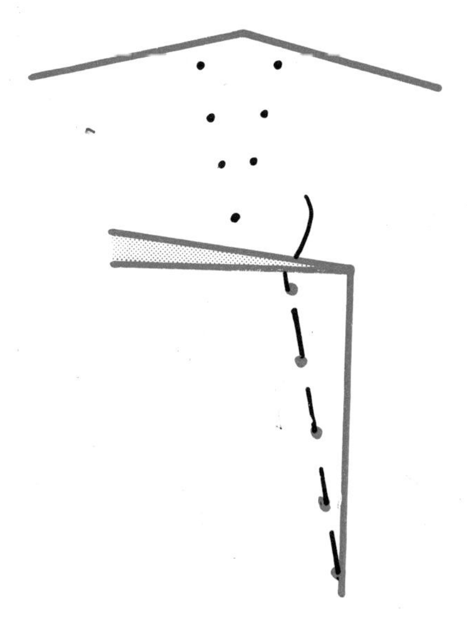

Shoulder darts. Press towards centre.

Underarm darts. Press downwards.

Dress waistline darts. Snip in the middle and neaten, so they can lie flat. Press towards centre.

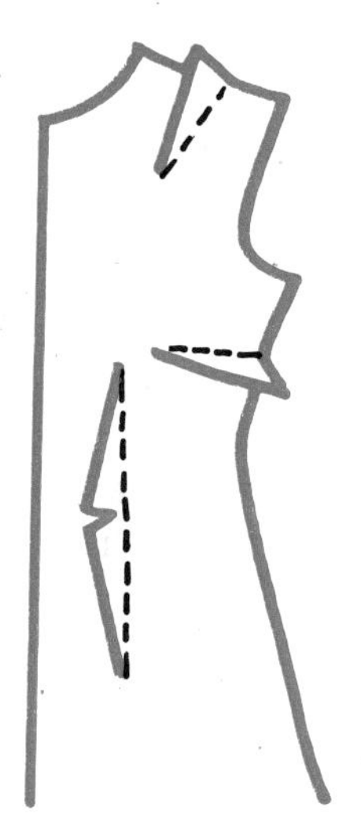

Skirt waist darts—press towards centre

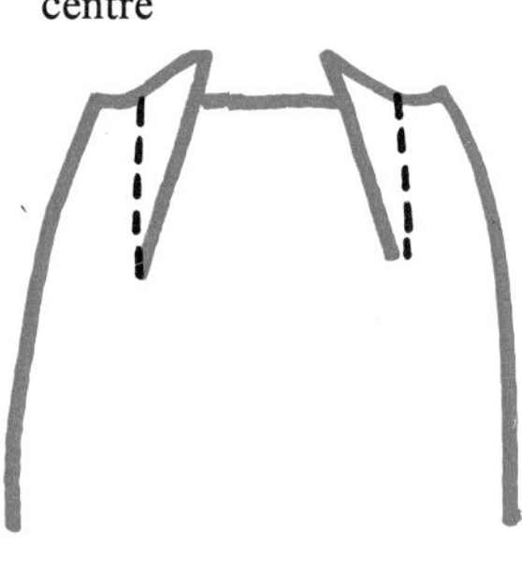

Darts on thick fabrics are slashed open, pressed flat, and neatened. This avoids bulges.

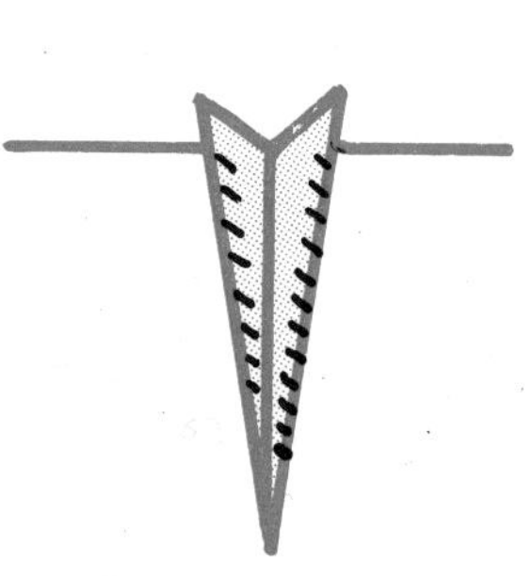

2. Pleats Straight folds of fabric from about 1″ to 3″ wide (2–7 cm), used to give room for movement, usually in skirts. Pleats take three times their finished width of fabric, as they form 3 thicknesses.

To make pleats, first turn up the hem—then tack or baste the pleats in place, and press them. This must be **very accurate** and usually on the straight grain of the fabric. Leave the tacking in until the garment is finished. Pleats may be machine-stitched part of the way down, if liked.

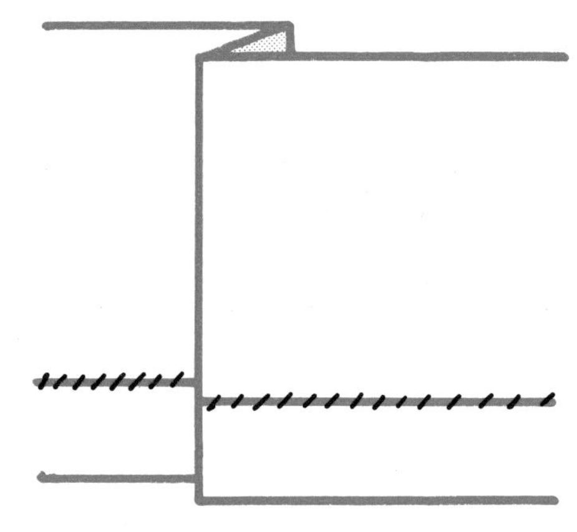

Knife pleat—wrong side, showing worked hem.

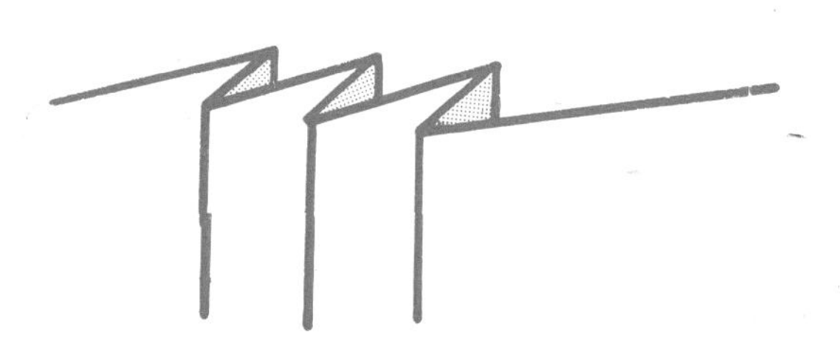

Group of knife pleats

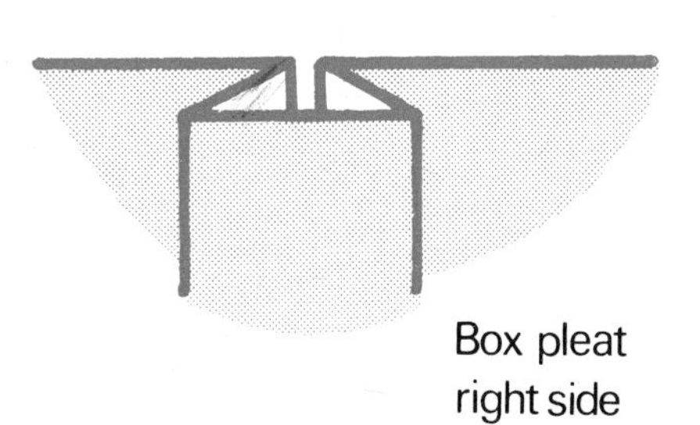

Box pleat right side

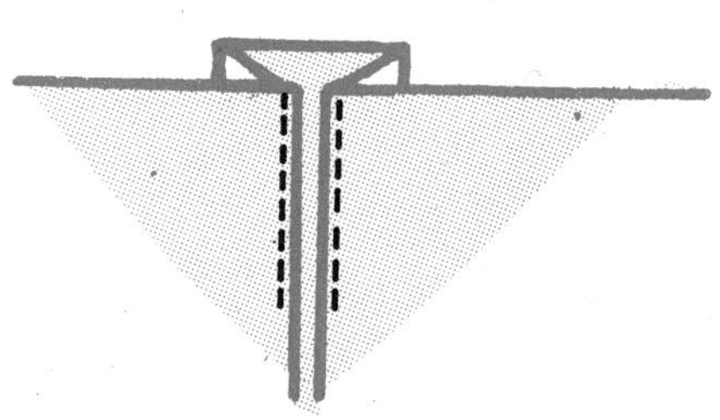

Inverted pleat, right side, stitched part way.

3. Tucks These are small pleats, from $\frac{1}{8}''$ to 1″ or more (2 mm to 2 cm), and stitched all the way. They may be made on the right or wrong side, and are used for shaping, for decoration, or on children's clothes for letting out as they grow. "Pin-tucks" are as thin as a pin. Press tucks **away** from the centre of the garment.

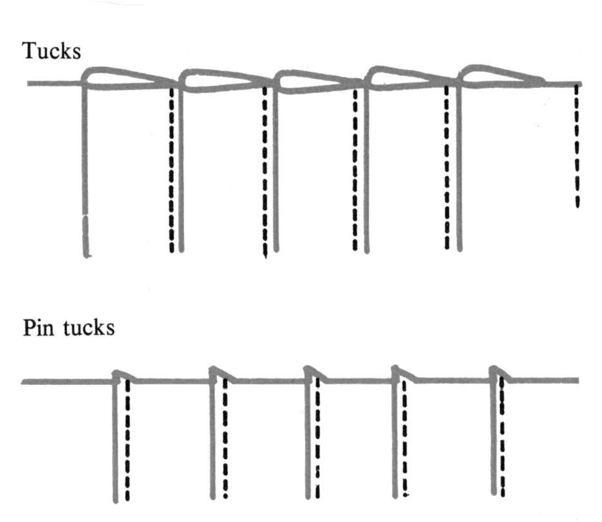

If gathering by machine, set the longest stitch you can, and loosen the top thread a little—the threads may be drawn up from **both** ends.

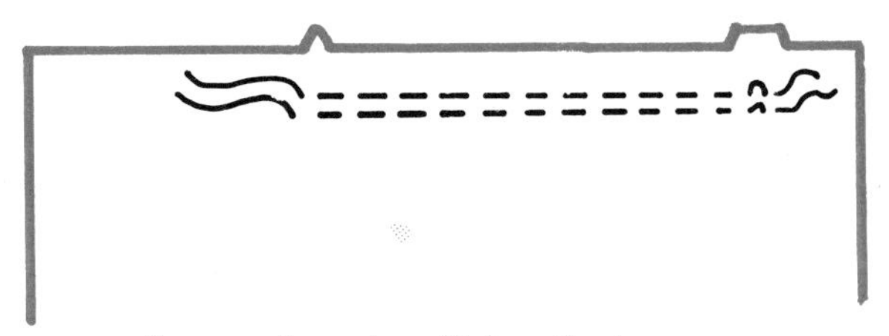

2 rows of running stitches, the lower one on the seam-line.

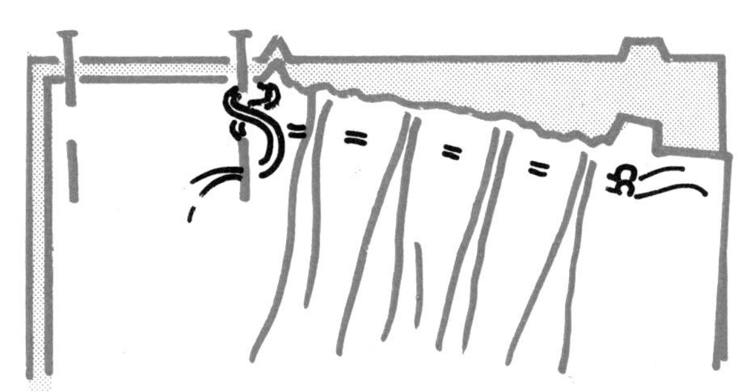

Gathers pulled up to fit, ready for tacking and stitching.

4. Gathers Used to give fullness at the top of sleeves, at cuffs, over the bust or at the waist. They look best on thin fabrics. The larger piece of fabric is "gathered up" and sewn to the narrower one, as the wider sleeve is gathered to fit the smaller cuff.

If you are gathering by hand, work a row of running stitches on the seam-line, and another $\frac{1}{4}''$ (0·5 cm) inside the seam allowance, starting with a double back-stitch and leaving the other ends loose. Draw up both threads together, evenly, to the length needed, and wind them round a pin to hold them. Then pin, tack and stitch the two pieces together, matching any notches. Gathering threads need not be taken out if they do not show.

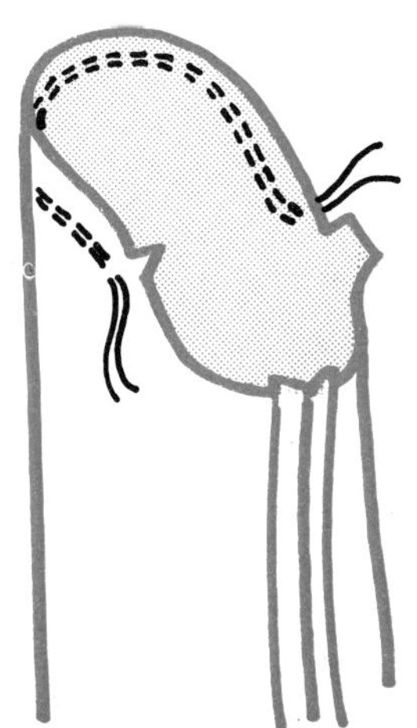

Gathering threads to "ease" or shape the head of a sleeve. Easiest by machine.

Shirring is using several lines of gathers for decoration—it may be done with elastic thread in the machine bobbin, and is useful for stretchy waistlines, etc.

Stay-stitching also helps the shape of your garment. It is a line of machine stitching, along a curved seam or neckline, on one thickness of fabric only, and just inside the seam allowance. It will not show, but will stop the seam from stretching.

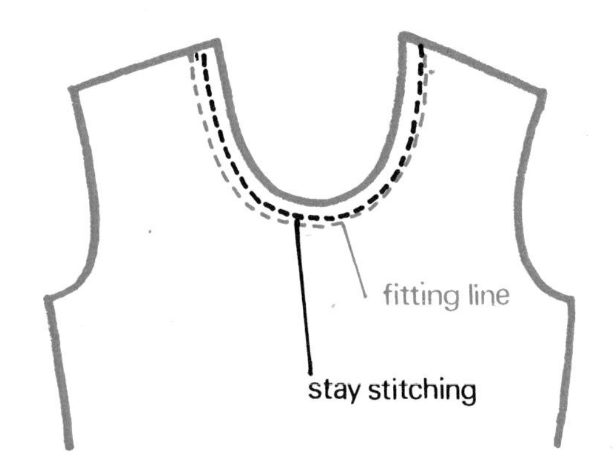

FITTING

Once the pieces have been shaped, tack together the whole garment, (except sleeves and collar) along the **fitting** (or stitching) line. Tack down centre front and centre back, if there is no seam there. This tacking line will show if the garment is hanging straight. Try the garment on, and check:

1. Is it a good fit, but not too tight? You should be able to sit and move comfortably, with the garment 2″ (5 cm) bigger round the hips than you are.
2. If it does not fit, alter it at the seams, first pinning and then tacking.
3. Pin in one sleeve, and check that the sleeve head sits nicely on the edge of the shoulder.
4. Check the hang of the whole garment. Does the centre front tacking hang quite straight down **your** centre front? And back? Do the sleeves hang straight?

Tack and fit accurately. The **seam allowance** is $\frac{5}{8}$″ (1·5 cm) unless the pattern says otherwise. A $\frac{1}{4}$″ (6 mm) smaller seam allowance taken at each edge of the four seams of these trousers, would make them 2″ (48 mm) bigger—**a whole size.**

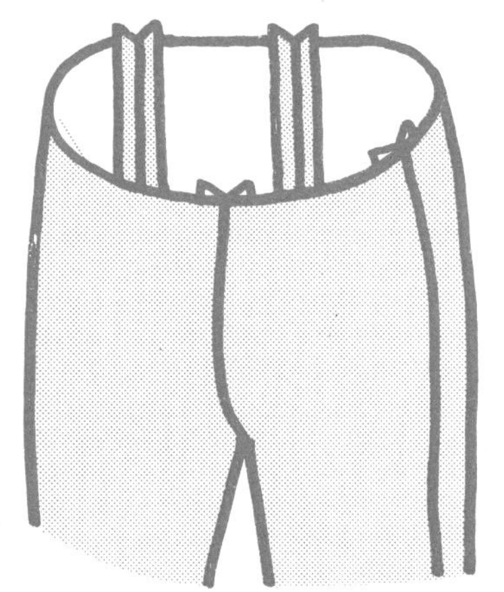

STITCHING THE SEAMS

Seams join the pieces of fabric together. It is best to stitch from the wider end of the piece, to the narrower end. This helps to stop the edges fraying.

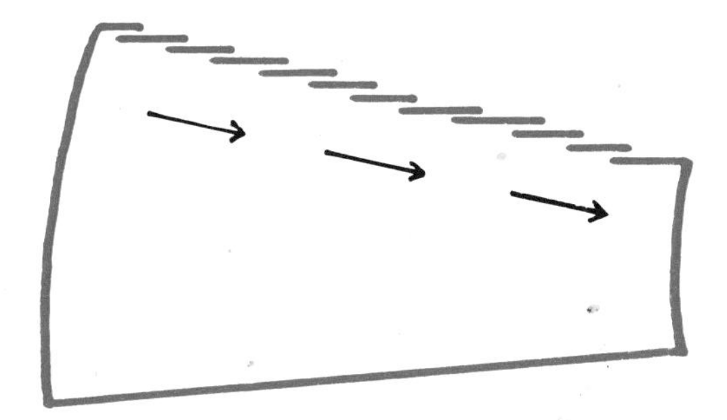

Hand-stitched seams

Running seam, with a back-stitch for strength after every few stitches. This is not a very strong seam, but suitable for dolls' clothes etc.

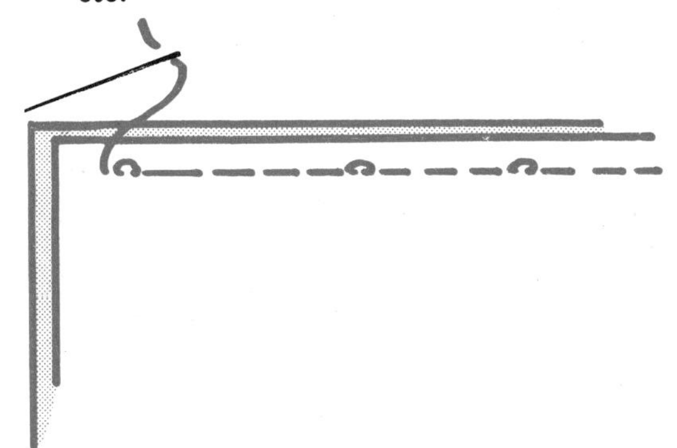

Oversewn seam, to join two hemmed edges, or selvedges. Use tiny stitches, very close together, and work from right to left. This is also a good way to attach lace, when it is called **whipping**.

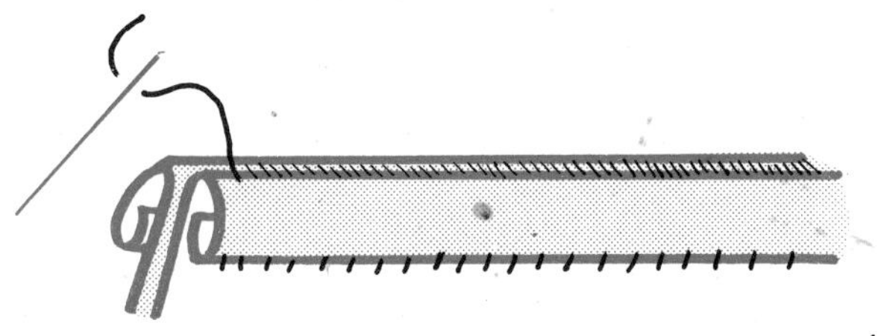

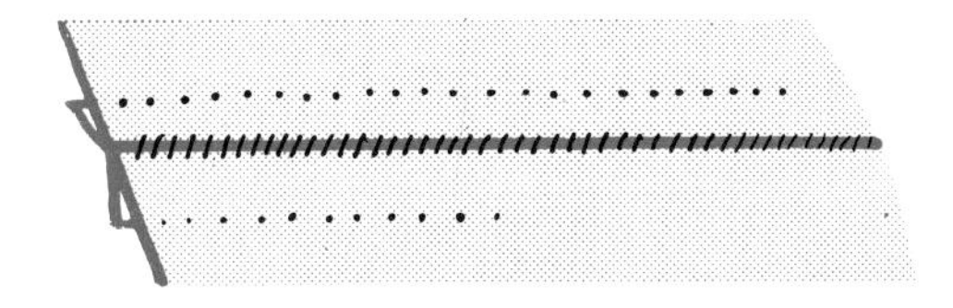

Machine-stitched seams Stronger and better for most garments.

French seam (Can also be sewn by hand.) Place **wrong** sides of fabric together and stitch $\frac{1}{4}''$ (0·5 cm) from the edge. Trim, press open, turn with wrong sides to **outside**, and tack. The second stitching is $\frac{3}{8}''$ (0·8 cm) from the first. French seams are useful for thin fabrics that fray easily, especially for underwear and children's clothes which need washing often. Not good for curved seams or corners.

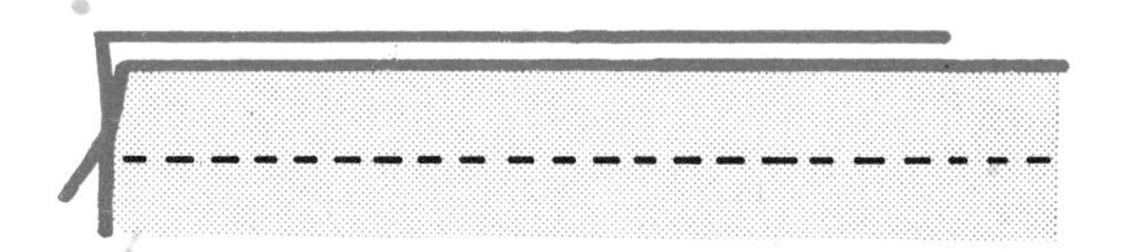

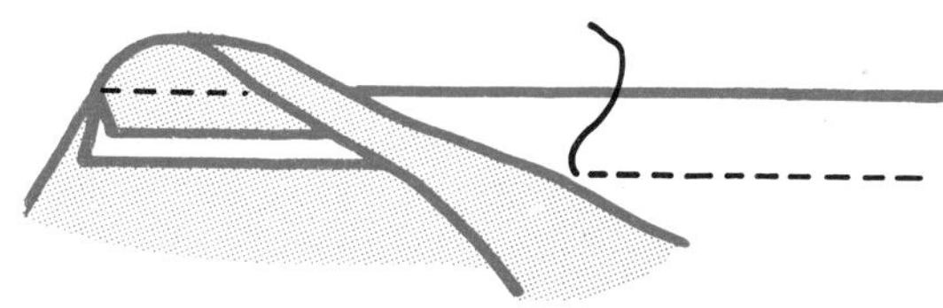

Machine fell (or double-stitched) seam Place **wrong** sides together, stitch along fitting line, and press edges towards back of garment. Trim the underneath edge to half its width, fold the upper edge over it, tack and machine. Useful for seams on pyjamas, or where a loose seam edge is not wanted; also for seams on jeans, etc, where stitching in a different colour shows up well.

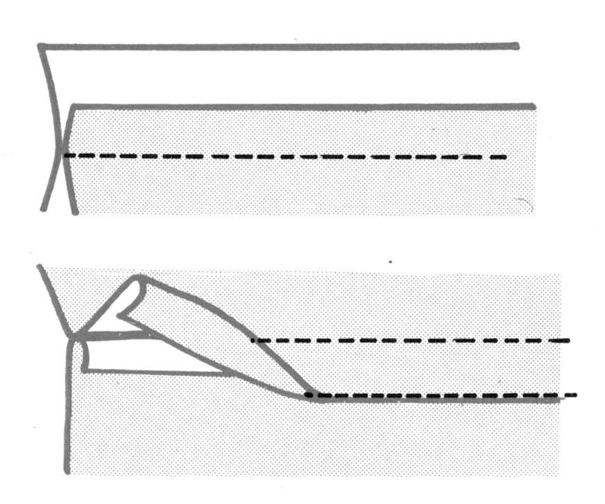

Overlaid seam This is used for decoration, or where a seam has a difficult corner or sharp curve. First, fold under the seam allowance of the top piece, and press. Mark the seam-line on the lower piece. Tack together, matching the folded edge to the marked seam-line. Stitch by machine—in a different colour if liked—$\frac{1}{8}''$ (0·3 cm) from the fold, through all thicknesses. This is **top stitching**. Neaten the raw edges by overcasting or loop-stitching together (see page 42).

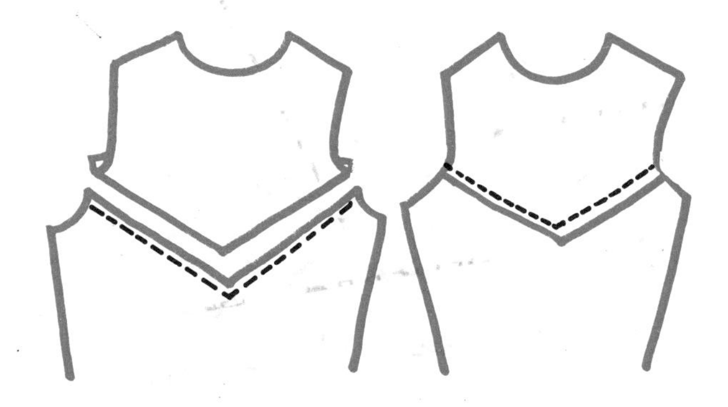

Flat seam (Dress-maker's seam) This is the easiest and most useful seam of all, but the raw edges need neatening after the seam is stitched, or they will fray out. With right sides together, take up the full seam allowance, tack, stitch and press the edges open. Now neaten the edges in one of these ways:

NEATENING

1. **Edge-stitching** Press under a narrow fold along each edge, and *machine-stitch* the fold. This finish is used for thin fabrics.

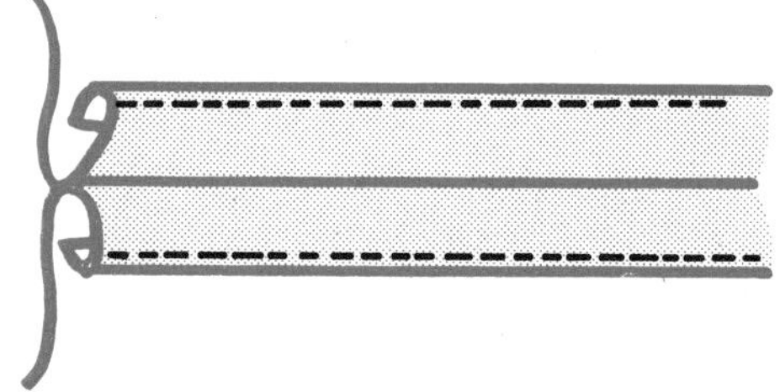

2. **Zig-zag machining** along each edge. This is for thick fabrics, and the edges are not doubled under.

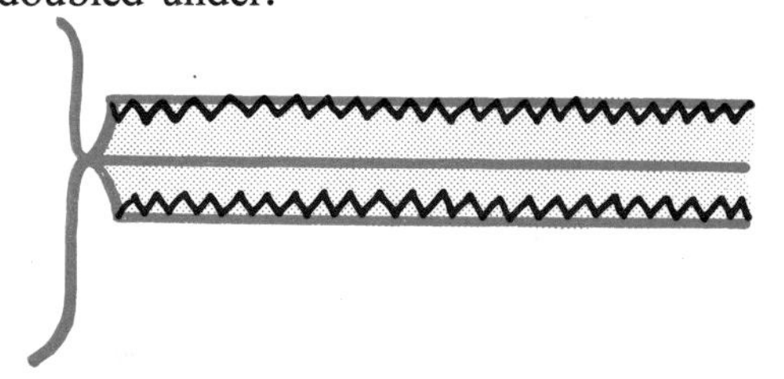

3. **Straight machining and overcasting by hand** along each edge, for thick fabrics that fray or stretch easily. **Overcasting** stitches should be about $\frac{1}{4}''$ (0·5 cm) apart, and not pulled up tightly.

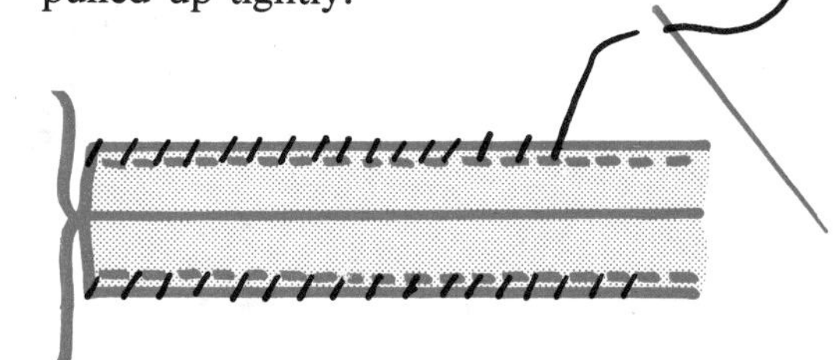

4. **Loop-stitching,** also for thick fabrics.

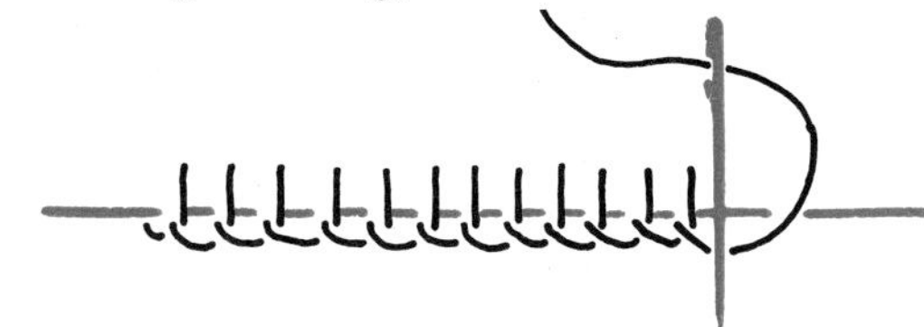

To neaten curved seams so that they lie flat, cut V-shapes out of the seam allowances, smooth off the corners, press open for thick fabrics, or to one side for thin fabrics, and **overcast by hand.** (It is very difficult to do this by zig-zag machining.) Do not neaten raw edges inside a collar, or where they cannot be rubbed.

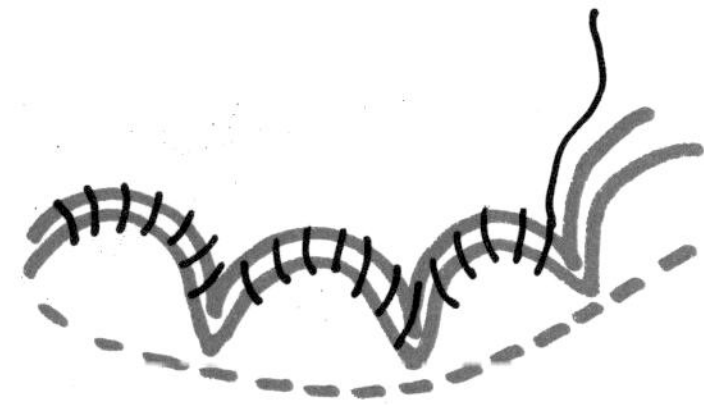

To neaten seams that cross, stitch and neaten the first pair of seams, place them together with the seams level, then do the crossing seam, and neaten its edges last of all.

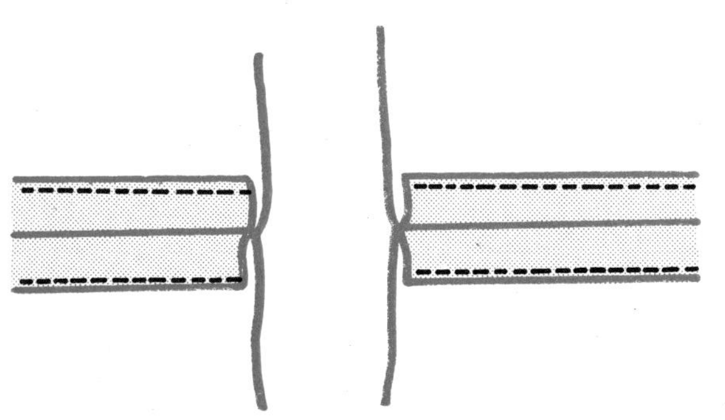

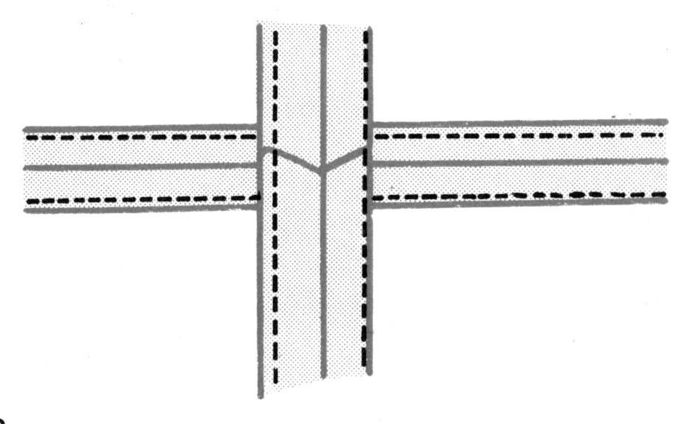

PRESSING

Press **every** part of the garment **as soon as you have sewn it**, because:

1 It is easier to work well on crisp, uncreased fabric, and
2. It is easier to press as you go than to press the whole garment when it is finished.

Always test the heat of the iron on a spare scrap of your fabric first—it is all too easy to burn a whole piece of your garment right out, on the sole-plate of an over-hot iron.

When pressing, do not slide your iron along—work along with heavy, slow, patting movements. ("Ironing" is quite different, see page 12.)

Press woollens, crêpes and dull-finished fabrics on the wrong side to stop them from becoming shiny.

Press woollens under a damp cloth.

Press along the straight grain of the fabric so that you do not pull it out of shape.

Press darts towards the centre of garments, or downwards.

Press seams open, or towards the back.

FACINGS, INTERFACINGS AND BINDINGS

These are different ways of strengthening, stiffening or finishing off the edges of garments at neckline, armhole or hem. Bindings and facings are sometimes used for decoration as well, so they may be of a different colour from the garment.

Facings are pieces of fabric shaped to fit and strengthen a neckline, armhole, etc. They also hide the raw edges of the fabric.

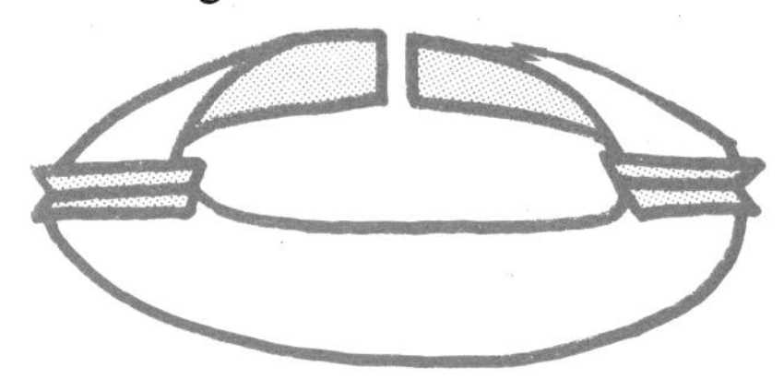

1. Front and back facings of a neckline stitched together.

2. Facings stitched to the neckline, **right sides** together.

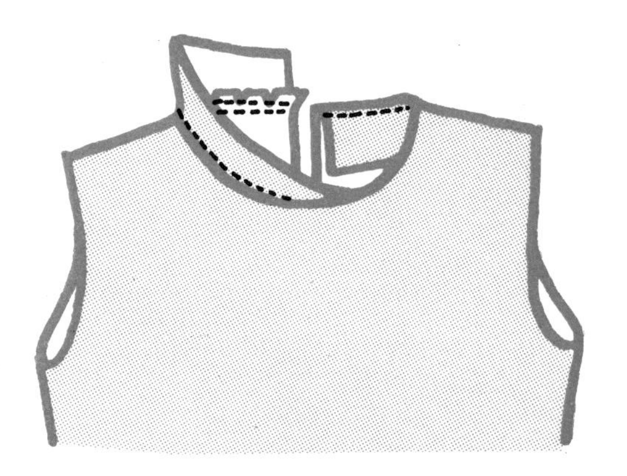

3. Facings opened out and **top-stitched**. Clip the raw edges so that they lie flat. Top-stitching is done on the right side of the facing, close to the first stitching, and **catching in all raw edges.** This stops the edges from rolling over to show the facing.

The loose edge of the facing should be neatened, but not the raw edges under it. Last of all, turn the facings to the inside and catch down with a few stitches at the seams.

Facings can also be used for scalloped hems on skirt or sleeve. With right sides together, stitch the scallops, making sharp points. Clip right into the points and trim the raw edges. Turn right side out and press.

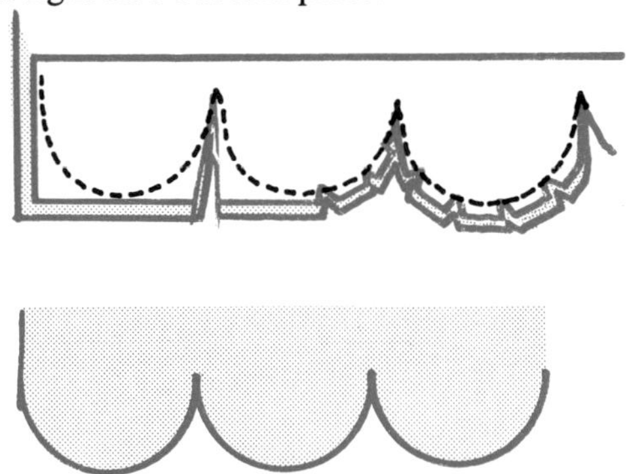

Finished scallops—right side.

Interfacings are used for stiffening collars, cuffs, necklines and front-buttoning edges of blouses or dresses. They are usually cut to the same shape as the facings. Interfacings for thin garments may be made of muslin or organdie; for thicker fabrics, use bonded interfacings such as **Vilene**.

Tack the interfacing to the **wrong** side of the garment piece. It is then held in place by the seams and facings.

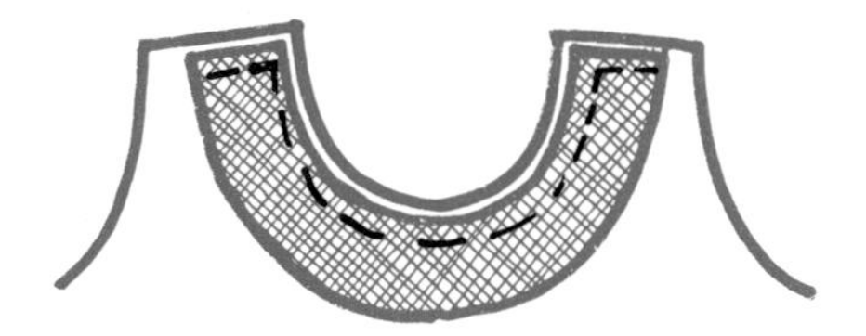

"Iron-on" Vilene can be ironed straight on to the facings, (but **not** on to the garment itself). For more about Interfacings, see "Collars", on page 48.

Cross-way strips and bias bindings

Strips of fabric cut "on the cross" or "bias", with the threads running diagonally, are useful for finishing off edges, especially curved ones. This is because bias strips will stretch to fit around corners.

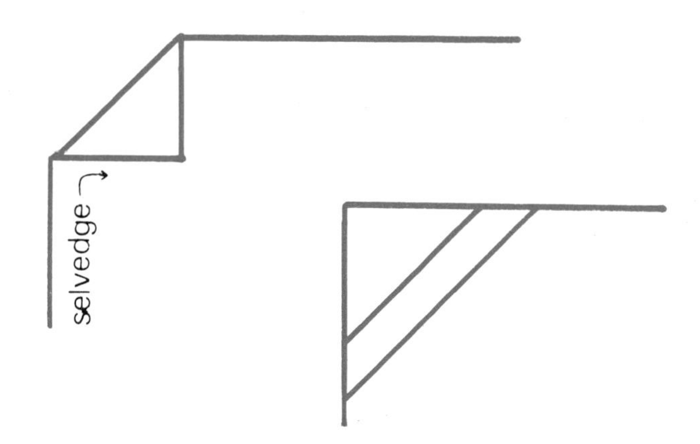

1. **To cut the strips:** Crease a corner of the fabric so that the selvedge makes a right angle with itself.

   Cut strips parallel to the crease, all of the same width. The width of a ruler (about $1\frac{1}{4}''$–3 cm) is useful.

2. **To join the strips:** Match two sloping ends, like this:

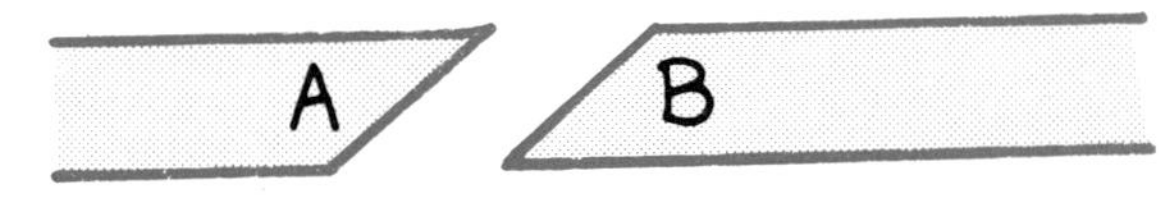

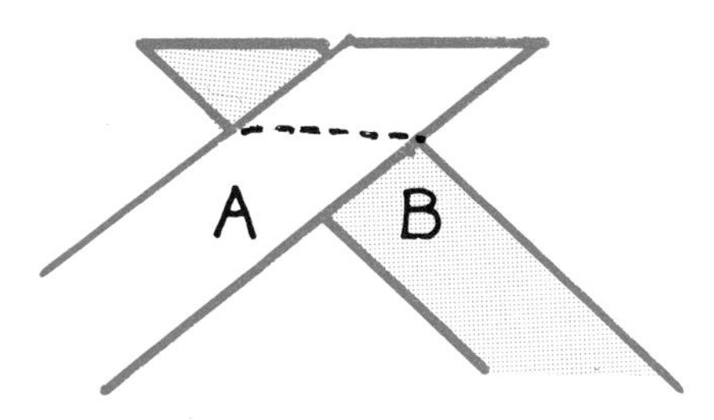

Turn A over and stitch to B with right sides together.

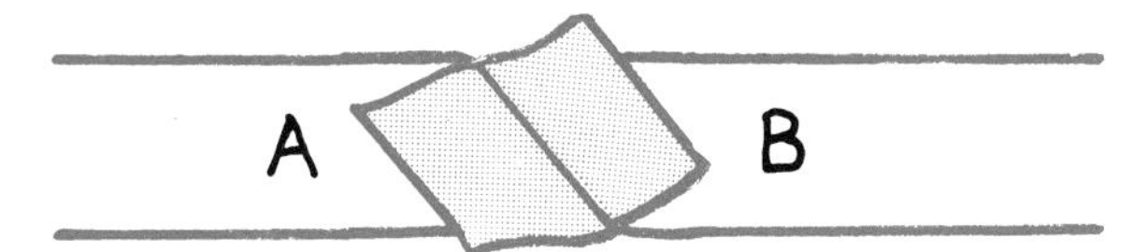

Press open and trim corners level.

3. **To use the strips of Bias Binding**, for example at the armhole of a sleeveless dress, machine-stitch the binding to the garment, **right sides** together, about $\frac{1}{4}''$ (0·5 cm) from the edge of the binding.

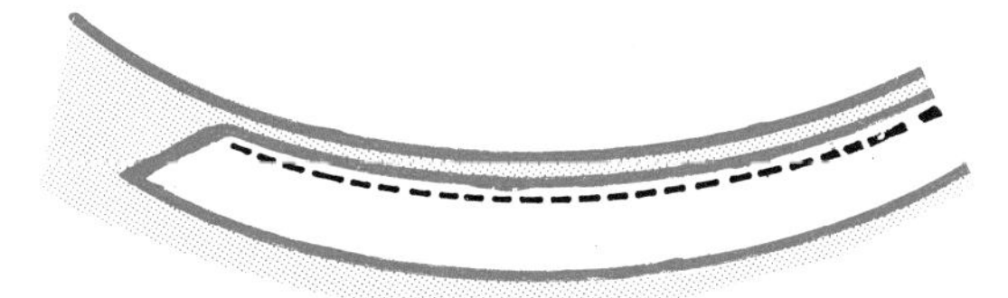

Ready-made binding may also be used, already creased where it should be stitched.

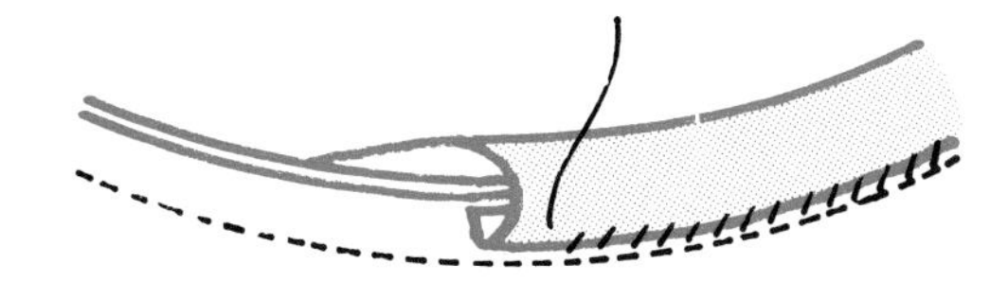

Turn binding over to the **wrong side**, fold in the loose edge about $\frac{1}{4}''$ (0·5 cm) and **hem** to the line made by the first stitching (see **hems**, page 53).

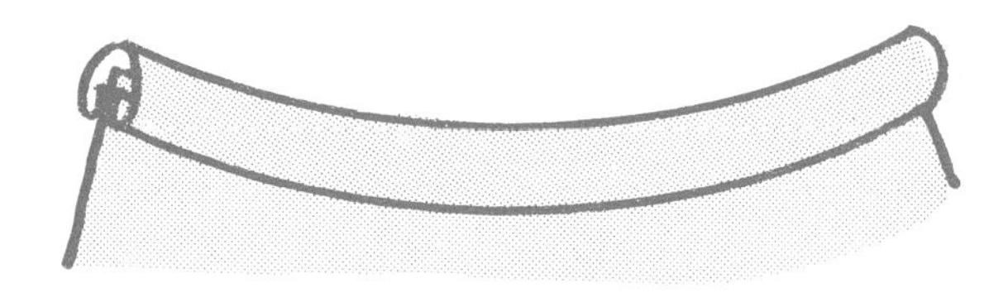

Finished binding—Right side.

OPENINGS

1. Faced openings, for instance on a neck edge, are made like other facings (p. 43) and turned to the inside of the garment.

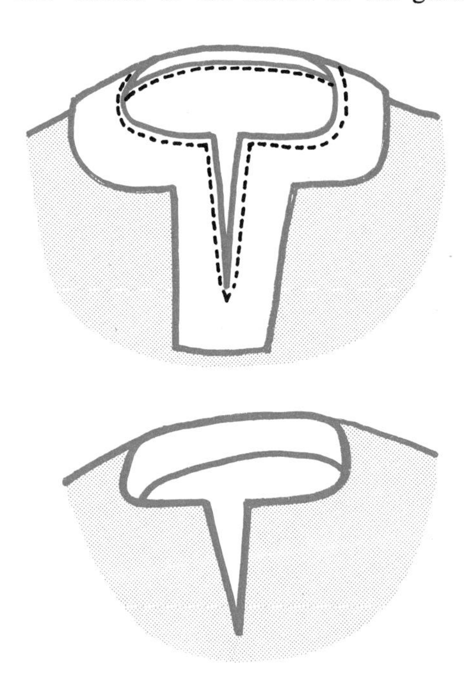

2. Bound openings, often used with a button and loop, are better for children's wear than facings, as there are no loose edges. (See above, under "Crossway Strips and Bias Bindings".)

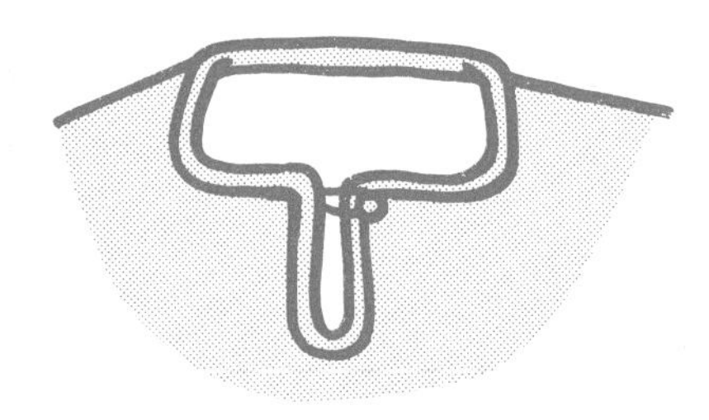

3. Continuous strip openings are mostly used for sleeves with buttoned cuffs. First, stay-stitch up one side of the opening and down

the other, in a V-shape. Slash the V open, right up to the point – – – – and spread the sides out.

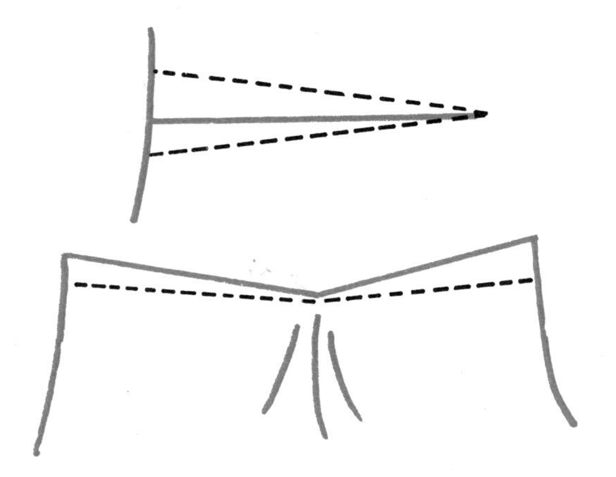

Cut a strip of fabric, on the straight grain, about $1\frac{1}{2}''$ (4 cm), or wider and just over twice as long as the opening. Stitch this along the whole slashed edge, right sides together, about $\frac{1}{4}''$ (0·5 cm) from the edge, along the stay-stitching.

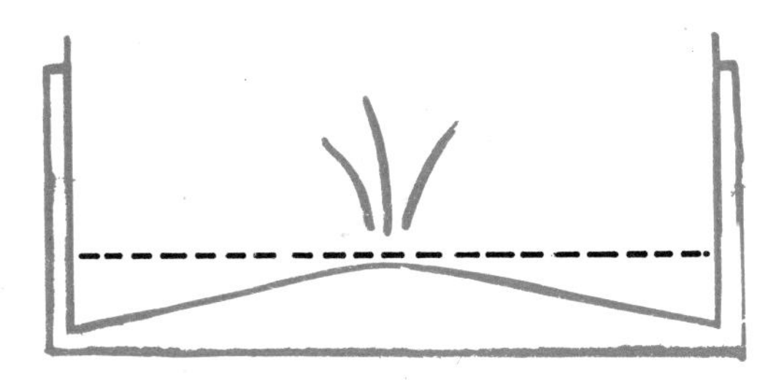

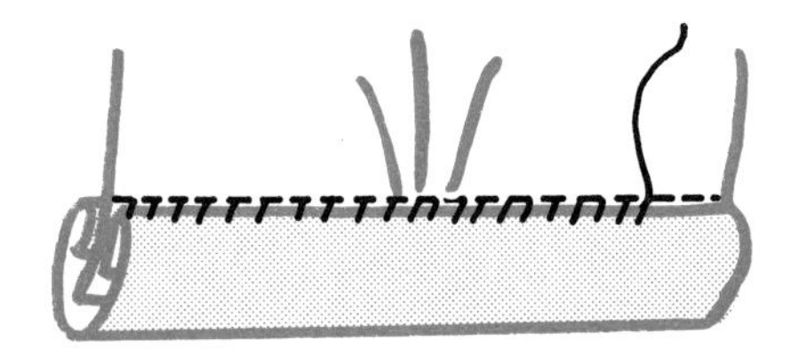

Turn the strip over to the wrong side of the garment. Fold in the loose edge of the strip $\frac{1}{4}''$ (0·5 cm), and hem just inside the first row of stitching. No stitches must show on the right side. On the wrong side, press the strip towards the front edge of the opening. Last of all, attach the cuff (see page 51).

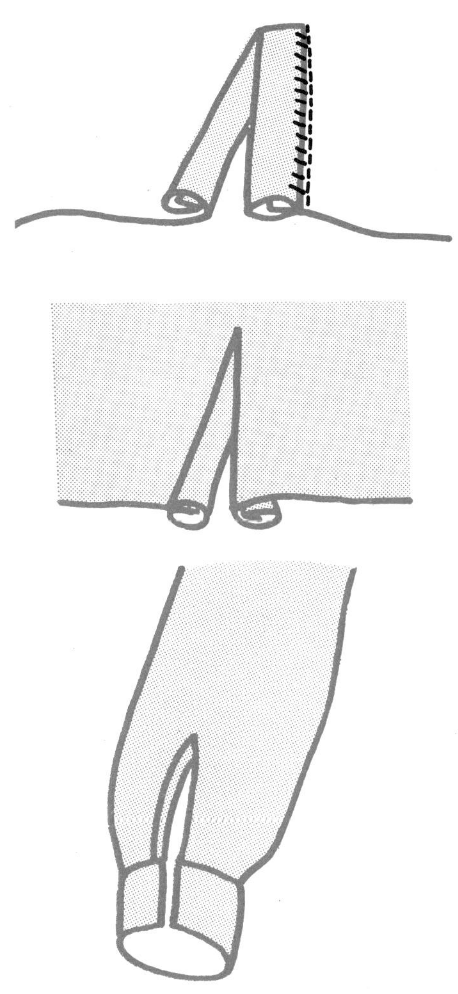

4. Zipped openings Zips are quick and easy to use, give a smooth fit and are safe to wash. They are made of nylon (for thin fabrics) or metal (for thick or heavy fabrics). If a metal zip sticks, rub a candle or a pencil over the teeth, and it will run smoothly.

Here is the easiest way to fit a zip, suitable for a neckline, skirt or trouser opening.

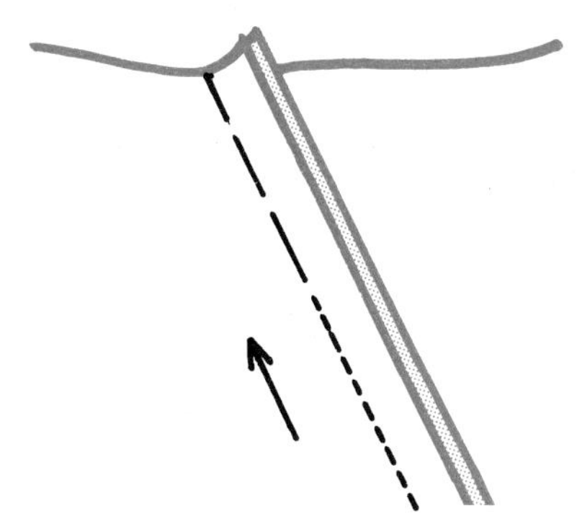

Machine-stitch the seam up to where the bottom end of the zip will be. Finish off the seam firmly, by turning the work round on the machine needle and going back right on top of the last few stitches. Now, with the **longest** possible machine stitch, start again from where you have just finished the seam, and sew right up to the top edge, still taking the full $\frac{5}{8}''$ (1·5 cm) seam allowance. (This is Machine Basting.)

Now press open the edges right along the whole seam.

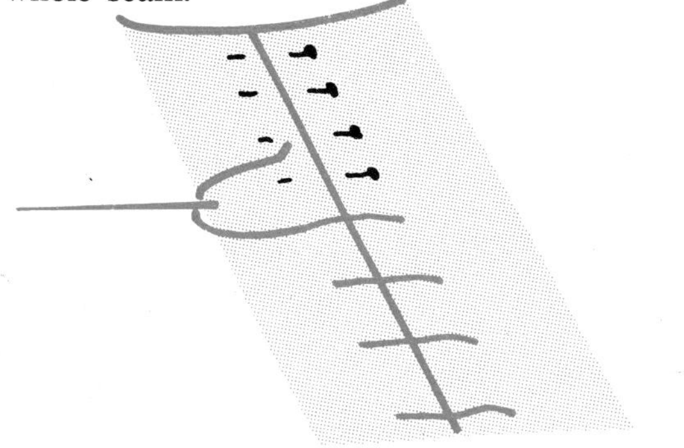

Lay the zip, right side up, on the table; lay the basted opening, right side up, on top of it. Pin the opening end of the zip **just below** the seam allowance at the top of the garment, then pin every inch, down to the lower end of the zip, keeping the zipper teeth (which you can feel through the basted seam) centred under the opening—or, if you like, $\frac{1}{4}''$ (0·5 cm) to one side of it, level all the way. The zip and the garment must lie quite flat, with no puckers.

Now baste firmly and remove the pins.

Turn to the wrong side. Fit the Piping Foot (or Zipper Foot) to the machine, and starting at the top end of the Zipper tape, stitch right down one side of the tape, **with the edge of the zipper foot in line with the edge of the tape**, to make sure you keep in a straight line.

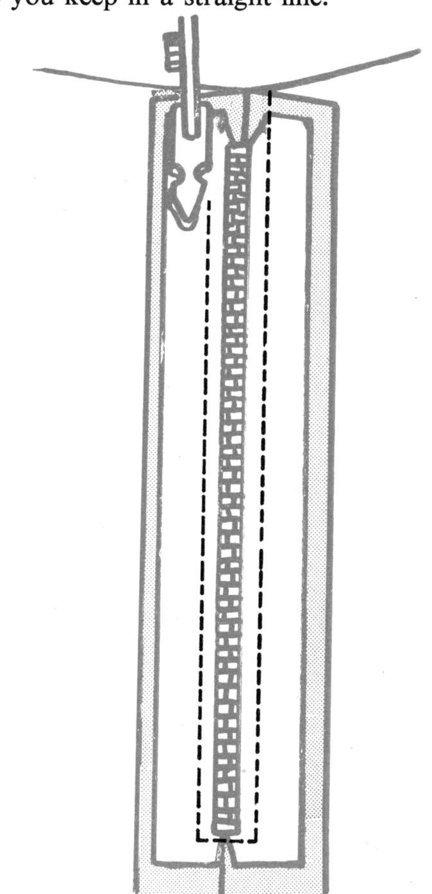

At the bottom, turn with the needle down, stitch across the tape below the end of the teeth, turn again and stitch up the other side of the tape. Take out the basting and machine-basting, and the zip will now open.

It is easier to fit the zip **before** sewing on the facings, collar or waistband at the top of the opening.

It is much easier to fit a back zip **before** sewing up the side seams of the dress.

COLLARS

To make your collar fit well and lie flat is one of the most difficult parts of dress-making—so first make sure that notches are cut and centres marked **accurately**, to give you exact guides. Then stay-stitch all round the neck edge of the garment, $\frac{1}{2}''$ from the edge, and snip **almost** down to the stay-stitching; this helps the neckline to stretch to fit the collar at the stitching line.

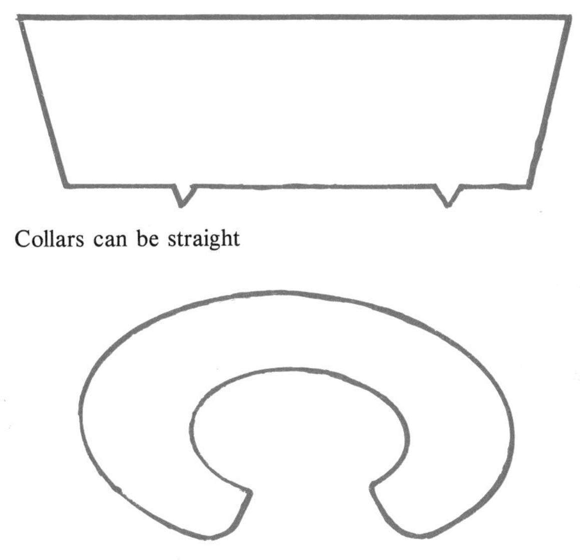

Collars can be straight

or shaped

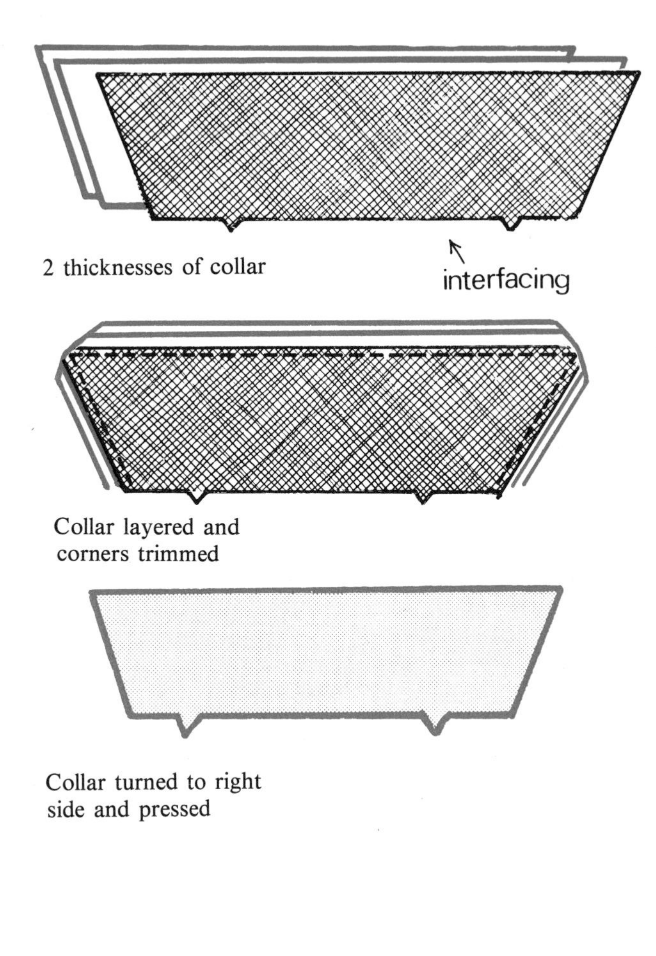

2 thicknesses of collar

Collar layered and corners trimmed

Collar turned to right side and pressed

For both sorts, cut out the collar twice from your fabric and once from interfacing. Place the two fabric pieces together, right sides inside, then place the interfacing on top. Tack all three together, leaving open the edge that will be stitched to the garment. Stitch by machine. Trim the interfacing almost down to the machine stitching, then trim one thickness of collar a little wider, and the other a little wider again. This is **layering**, and is to get rid of any extra fabric that would make the collar edges bulky. Trim closely across the corners. Cut V-shapes out of seam edges where they are curved (See p. 42).

To fit a collar with facings down the opening edge of blouse or jacket Open out the front facings and lay the collar in place on the right side of the garment. Fold the facings back over the right side, so that their ends come up to the shoulder seams and cover the ends of the collar. Pin and tack right across, being careful to keep the garment, facings and collar exactly in place. Then lay a piece of bias binding along the stitching line between the shoulder seams, easing a little as you go, and tack it in place. Machine right across.

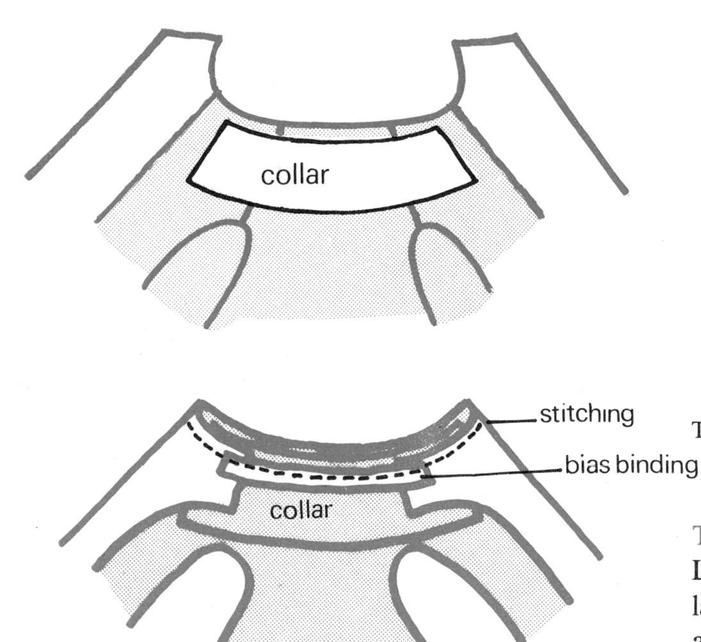

Facings folded back. Bias binding placed on stitching line

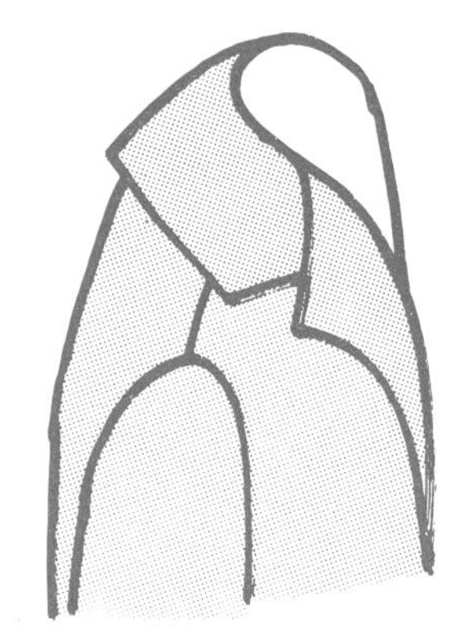

The finished collar.

Now turn the facings over to the inside. The bias binding will turn over with them. Hem the loose ends of the facings to the shoulder seams, and the loose edge of the binding to the back neck of the garment.

To fit a collar without facings

Lay the collar on the right side of the garment, lay a piece of bias binding, right side down, along the whole length of the collar. Pin, tack and stitch the whole length. Trim the seam edges of collar and neckline into neat layers, turn down the bias binding to hide them, tuck in the ends, and hem.

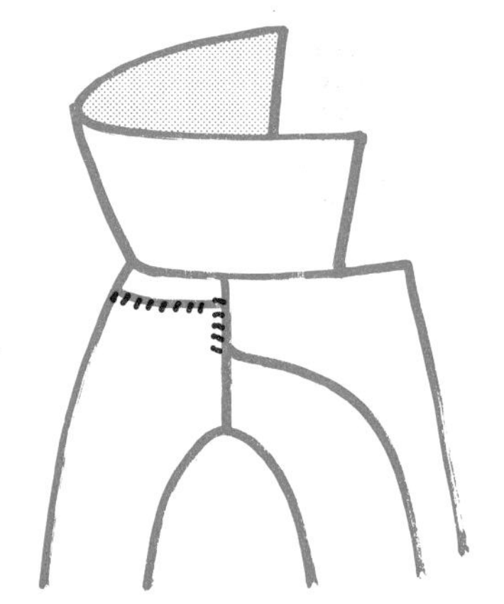

Bias binding and facings hemmed down.

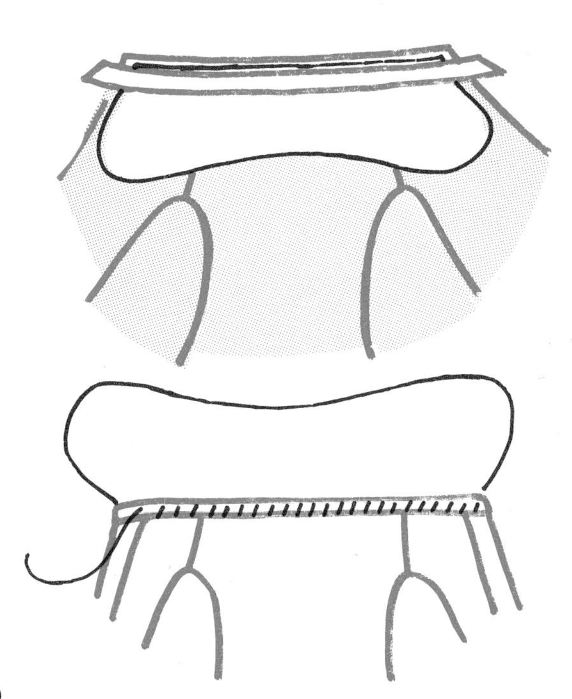

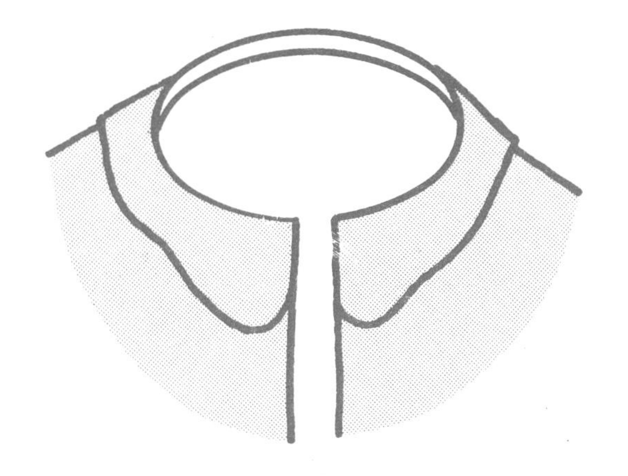

SLEEVES AND CUFFS

Sleeves

To hang straight, sleeves **must** be cut exactly on the straight grain, with the warp threads running up and down the sleeves. The top ("head") of a sleeve will seem too wide to fit the armhole—it has to be gathered before setting into the garment, so that there is plenty of room for shoulder and arm movements.

First, stitch the shoulder and underarm seams of the garment. Then run two gathering threads round the upper part of the sleeve-head, leaving the ends of the threads loose.

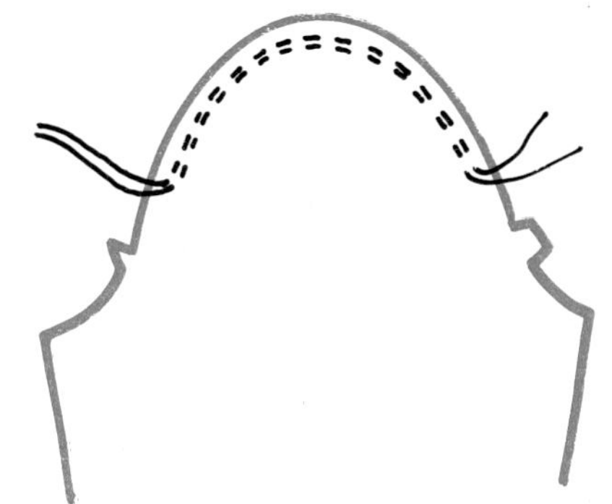

Now stitch the sleeve seam. (It is best also to finish off the lower end of the sleeve **before** setting it into the garment.)

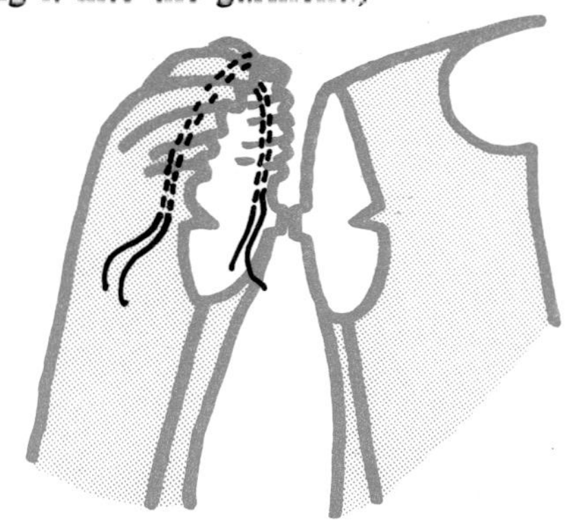

Place the sleeve against the garment, right sides outside, to check that right and left sleeves go to their own armholes. The single and double notches must match.

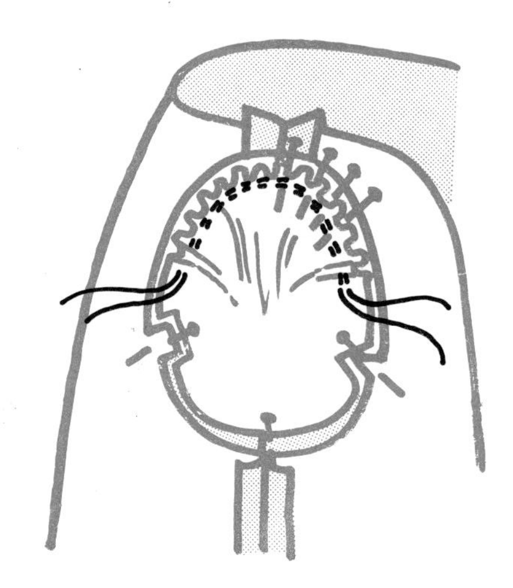

Now turn the garment inside out **over** the sleeve; the sleeve stays the right side out. Pin **underarm seams** together, **head of sleeve** to **shoulder seam**, and **match the notches**. Pull up the gathering threads to fit, and use plenty of pins to spread the gathers. Turn to the right side to check that the gathers are even and the sleeve sits well. Now tack along the fitting line, from the underarm seam up to the shoulder and down again the other side. Stitch as in diagram, so that the sleeve material is next to the machine foot and the bodice material below.

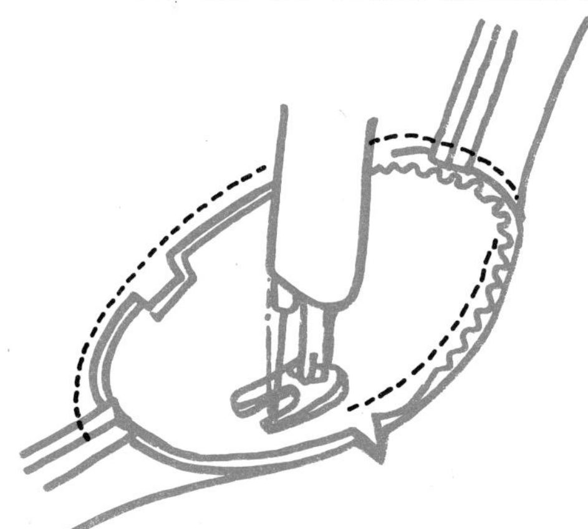

Trim raw edge and neaten. Thin fabrics are best neatened with bias binding; thick ones with zig-zag machining through both thicknesses. Press the finished armhole seam towards the sleeve.

Cuffs are interfaced and made up in the same way as straight collars. Then stitch the outside layer of the cuff (with the interfacing) to the gathered sleeve, right sides together.

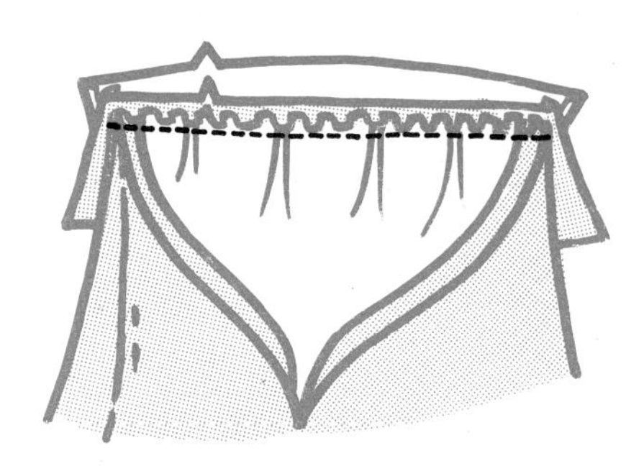

Now turn over the inside layer of the cuff and hem to the wrong side of the sleeve, just inside the first stitching, so that no stitches will come through to the right side.

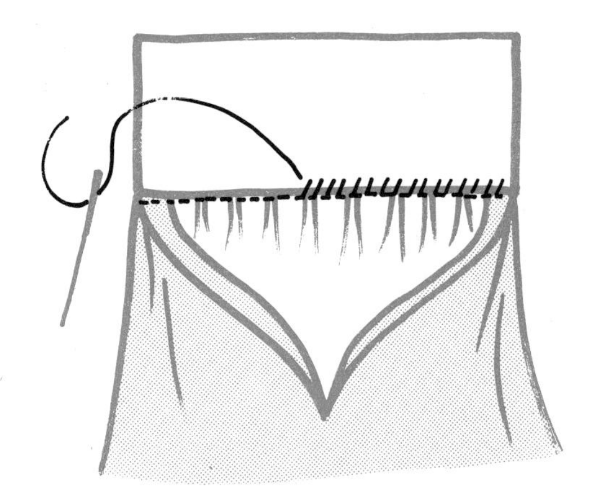

SKIRT OR TROUSER WAIST FINISHES

With belting Place belting or Petersham ribbon inside the skirt or trouser waist, so that the lower edge of the belting lies just below the waist fitting line. Tack and stitch to the fitting line. Neaten the raw edges round the waist by stitching seam binding over them. Fold belting down to the inside.

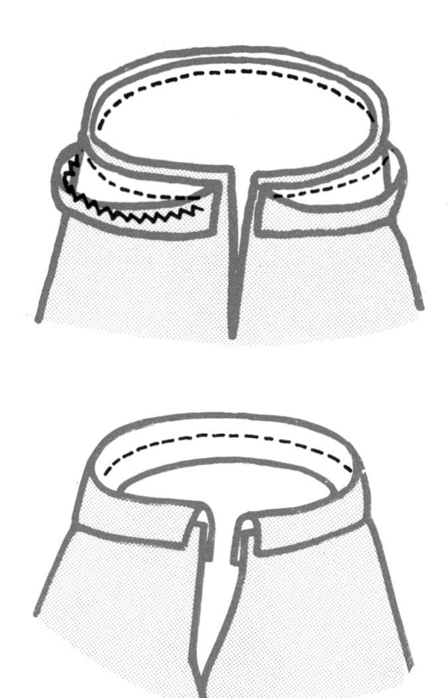

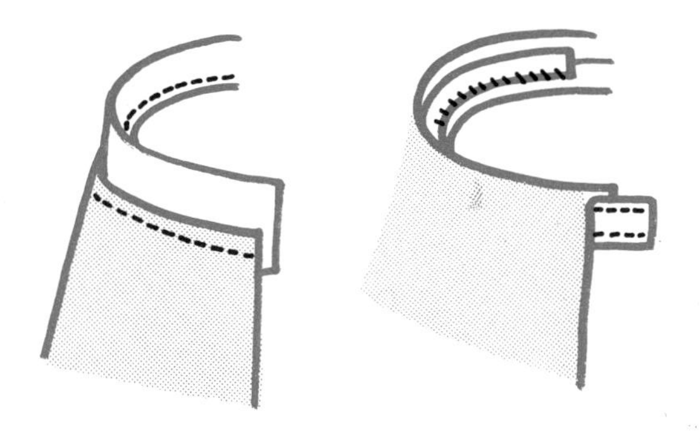

With a waist-band This is a fabric strip folded double, and strengthened with interfacing. Iron-on **Vilene** is good for this. Fold the right sides together, and stitch the ends, leaving the seam allowances free. Turn right side out and press.

Now stitch the outside layer of the waistband to the fitting line of the skirt or trouser waist, **right sides together**. Neaten the other edge by zig-zag machining or overcasting. Slip this edge inside the waist. Tack and **top-stitch** from the outside exactly along the seam line. This stitching will not show, as it will sink into the seam.

HEMS

Turn up and pin the same amount of hem all round the garment. Try it on, and get a friend to check with a yardstick that it is the same distance from the floor all the way round. If not, pin again. Stand evenly on both feet and do not bend forward to look while your hem is being pinned. Tack the fold all round, matching at the seams, and trim the turning to an even width—about 2″–2¼″ (5–6 cm). Try on again. Then finish the hem in one of these ways:

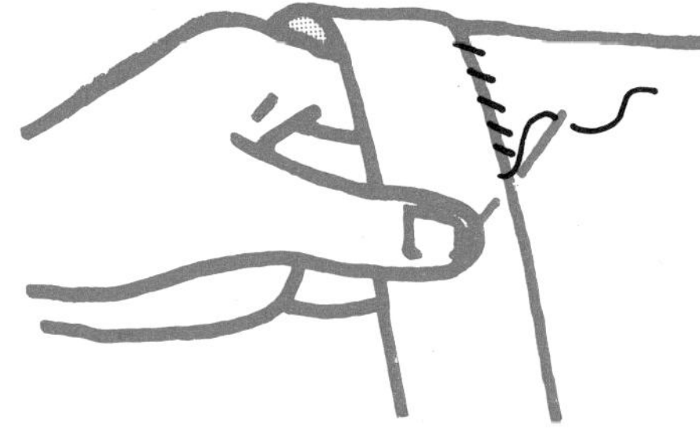

For thin fabrics Turn in a narrow "lay" (or fold) and hem, holding the garment like this.

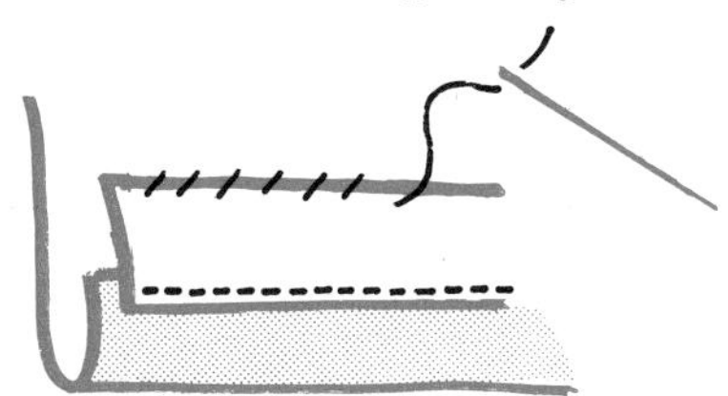

For thick fabrics Machine-stitch seam binding along edge, then hem to garment.

For curved hems, circular skirts Gather the edge to fit, and finish with bias binding machined on the gathered edge and hemmed to the garment.

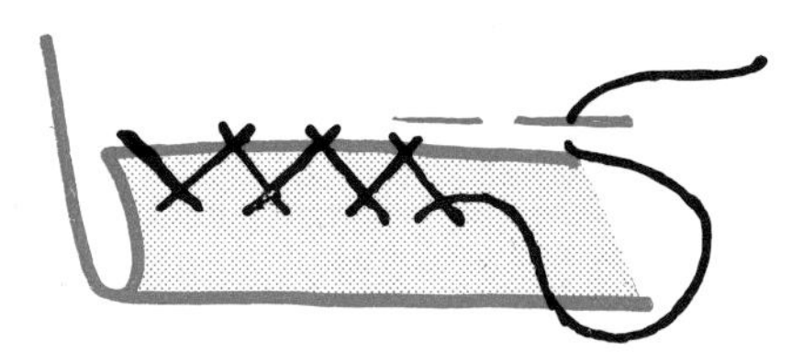

For thick or stretch fabrics Herring-boning with small stitches, worked from left to right. This is useful for jersey.

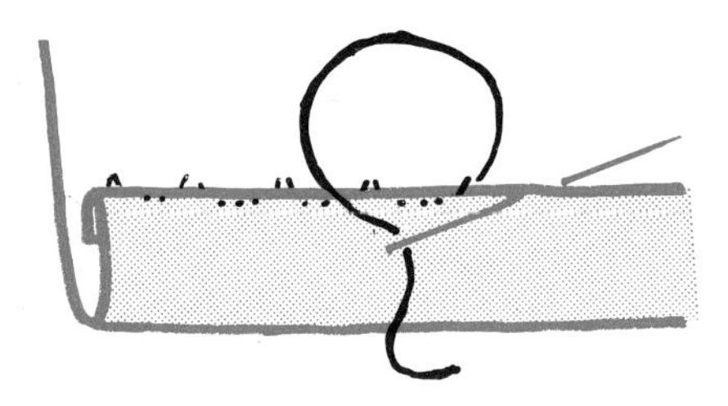

Slip-hemming shows less on the right side Take up only two or three threads at each stitch, and run the needle along *inside* the fold, between stitches, 4 stitches to the inch is small enough.

Always hem loosely—then no line will show on the right side.

PATCH POCKETS

Five easy steps

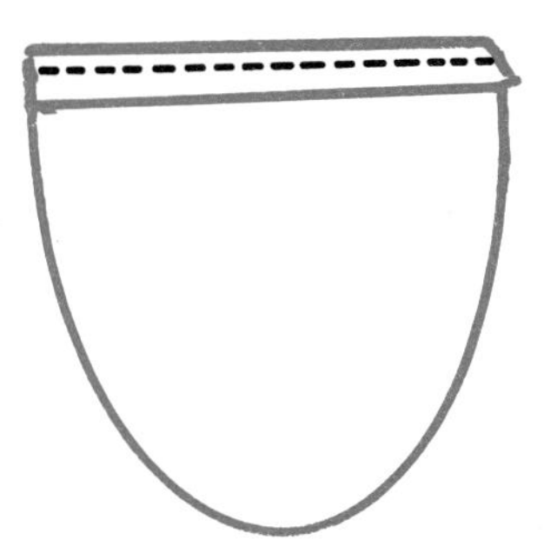

Turn $\frac{1}{4}''$ (0·5 cm) along top of pocket to wrong side and stitch.

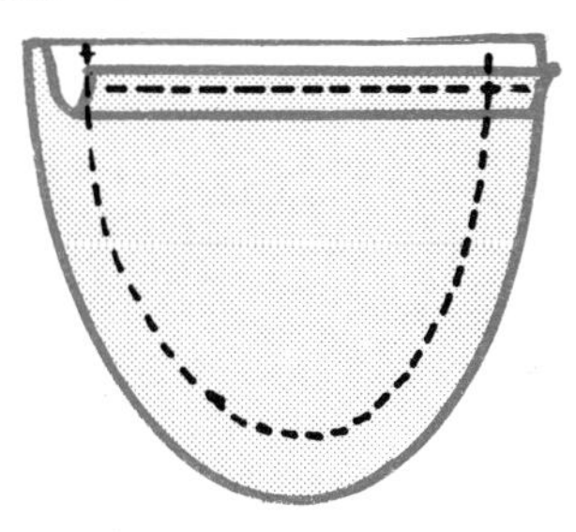

Press a fold about 1″ (2·5 cm) at top of pocket, to **right** side. Stitch round sides on stitching line.

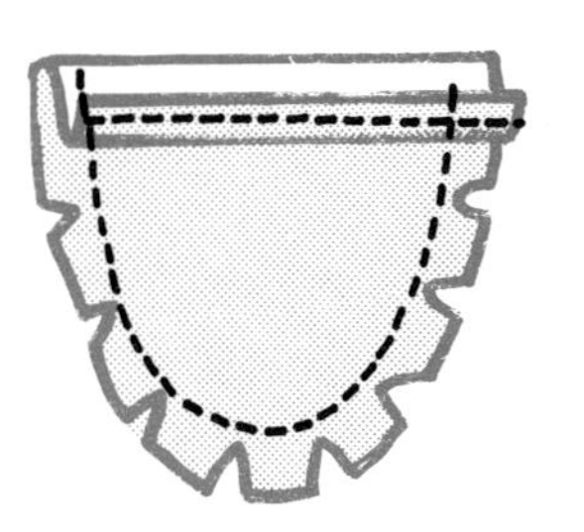

Clip curves.

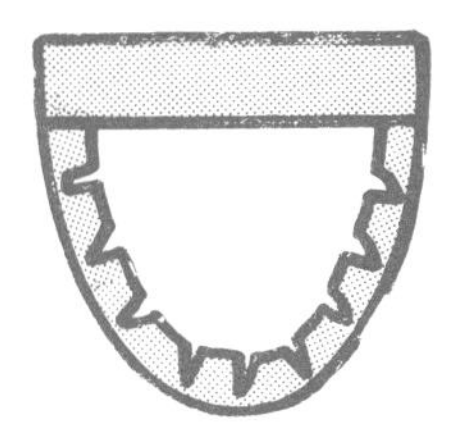

Turn pocket top to wrong side—press edges under, along stitching.

Finished pocket, right side—**top-stitch** to garment, finishing off the top corners by stitching little triangles or squares to strengthen.

Bound buttonholes, used for thick fabrics. Cut a patch of fabric, about 2″ (5 cm) square, on the straight grain, for each buttonhole. Pin the patches, right side down, on the right side of the garment, making sure they are spaced evenly. Do **not** catch in the facing along the edge of the garment.

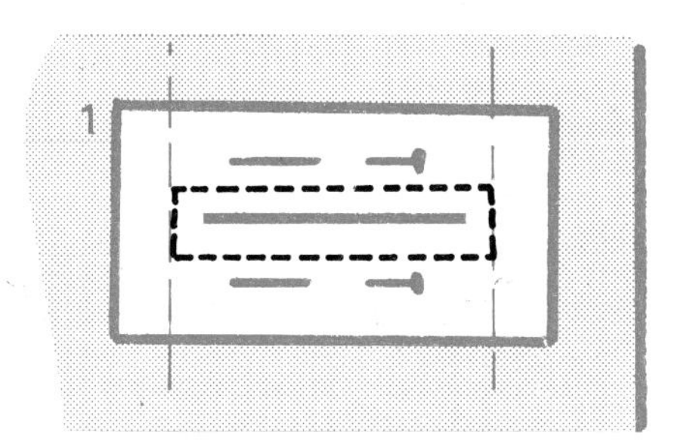

1. Mark the ends of the buttonholes with two lines of tacking, which will also hold the patches in place. Mark with tailor's chalk or pencil the exact position of each buttonhole between the two lines of tacking. Stitch all round the buttonhole with a small machine stitch, $\frac{1}{8}$″ above and $\frac{1}{8}$″ (about 0·3 cm) below the marked line.

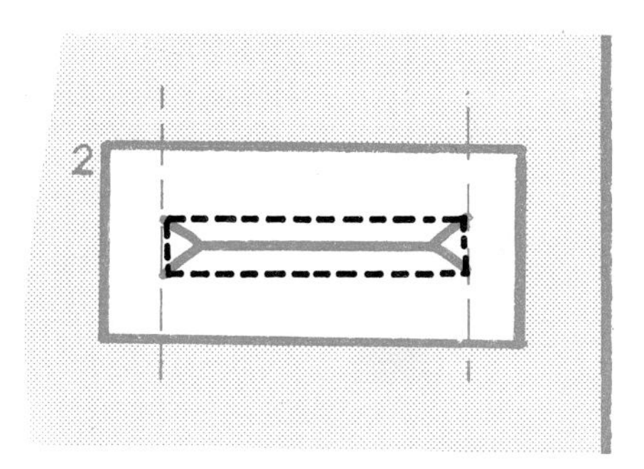

2. Cut open the buttonhole through both thicknesses, clipping little triangles right into the corners.

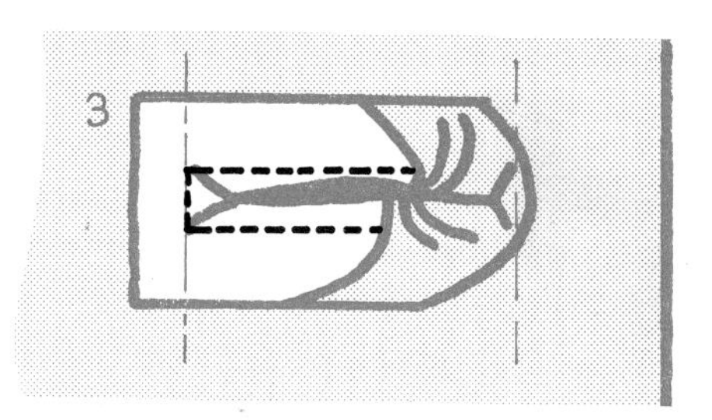

3. Push the patch right through the cut buttonhole, to the wrong side.

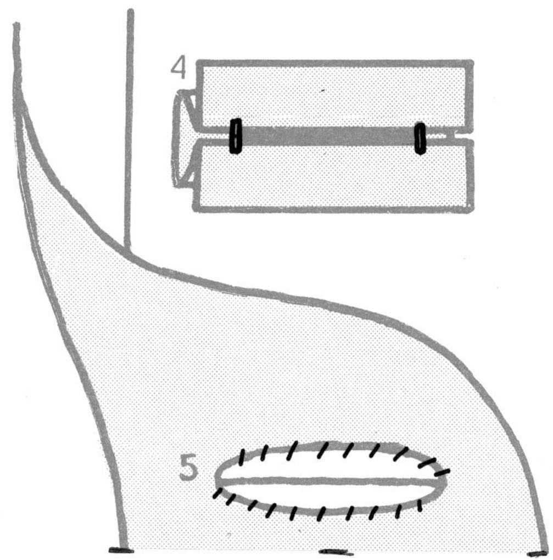

4. On the wrong side, pull the folds of the patch sideways and level along the buttonhole. Tiny pleats will form at each end—stitch these down by hand as shown, catching in the little triangles.

5. Now tack the facing into place behind the buttonhole. From the **right** side, cut through the facing exactly behind the buttonhole. Fold in the cut edges very narrowly, and hem to each edge of the buttonhole.

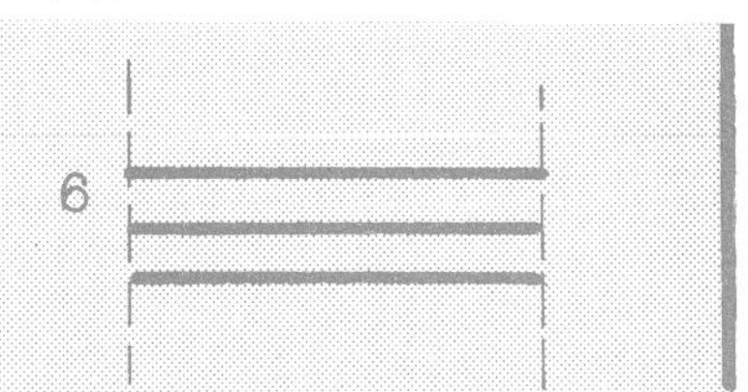

6. The finished buttonhole, right side.

For all buttonholes, mark the position exactly. Keep at equal distances and in a straight line.

Handworked buttonholes For thin fabrics.

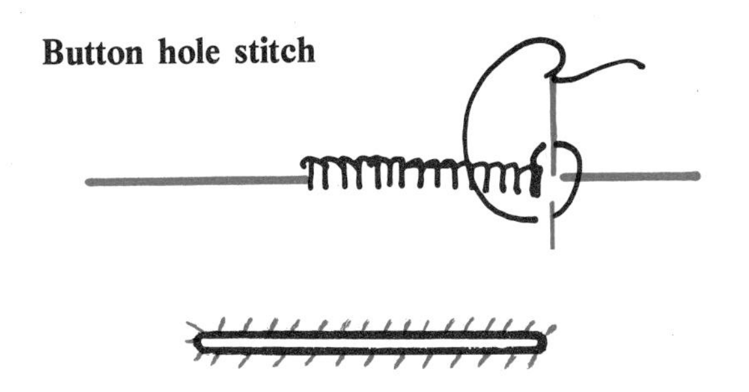

Cut slit for buttonhole, and overcast to stop fraying.

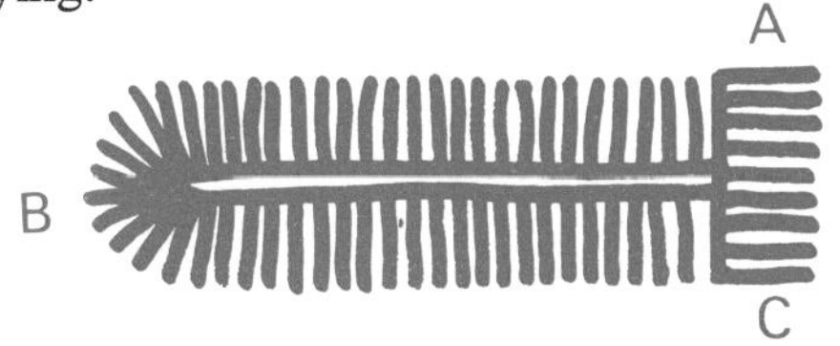

Buttonhole stitch from A, inside end of buttonhole, to B, end nearest garment edge, and back the other side to C. Then across end. Slip thread under a few stitches to finish off.

Machine buttonholes For all fabrics.

Use Buttonhole Foot on Swing-Needle machine and follow carefully the machine instruction book. Width of end stitches is just over double the width of stitches on sides. Be careful not to catch the first side in when stitching the second. Slit open with seam-ripper, working always from ends to middle. Pull ends of thread to the wrong side, thread them into a needle, and run them away between the two thicknesses of fabric.

Buttons Buttons will have holes on top, or else a shank underneath for the hole.
For the shank type, sew to the garment with about 6–8 stitches, not pulled tightly, in double thread. Finish off safely with 2 loop-stitches at the back.
For buttons with holes, and no shank, the stitches must be loose enough to let the button stand $\frac{1}{8}''$ away from the fabric. After stitching through the holes, wind the thread three or four times round the "stalk" to avoid wear on the threads holding the button. Then finish off on wrong side.
Buttons should be sewn to double fabric.

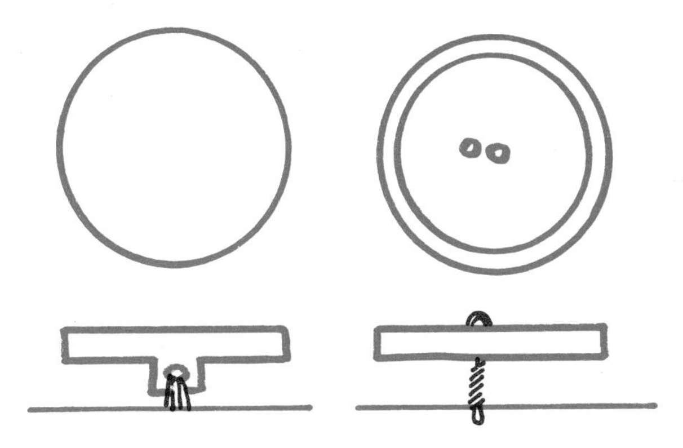

Hooks and eyes Sew on very firmly, including round the neck of the hook. Large hooks and bars are useful for skirt and trouser waist fastenings. Loop-stitched bar-tacks can be used instead of metal ones—they show less. Long bar-tacks can be used as belt-carriers.

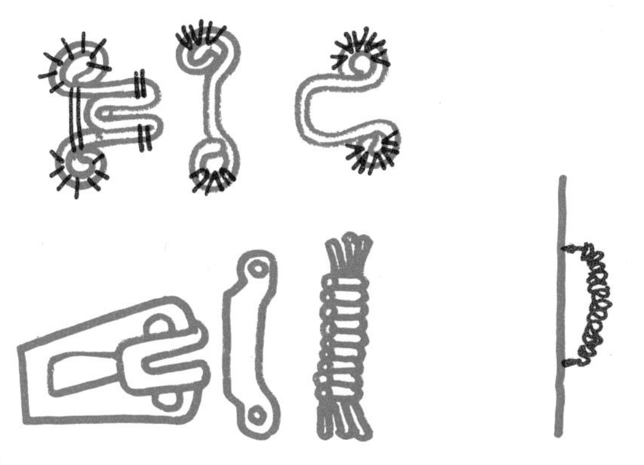

Press studs The half with the knob should be sewn to the overlap side of the garment; the half with the hole is sewn to the underlap. That way, they do not leave marks on the outside when ironed. While stitching, hold press studs in place with a pin through the tiny centre hole.

Velcro is useful for aprons, bibs, sportswear, etc. The hooked side faces away from the body; the soft, fluffy side towards the body, on the overlap. Press to fasten—pull apart to open. Machine in place, round all four sides of the tape; patches 1″–2″ long (2·5–5·0 cm) are quite big enough for most fastenings. Velcro is bought by the inch.

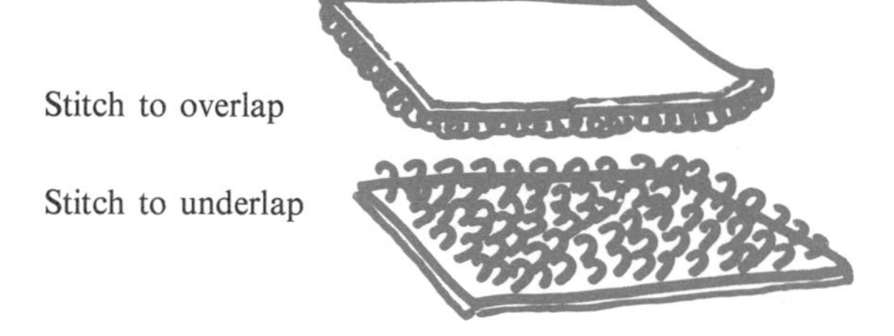

Zip fasteners See page 46.

6 PASSING YOUR EXAMINATION

TWELVE TIPS FOR SUCCESS

Tackling an Exam the right way can add at least 20 marks in 100 to your score.

1. Revising Revise by reading this book right through, and thinking of the **reasons** for these rules of dress-making. Once you understand **why** clothes are made like this, you will not forget. Do not try to learn by heart.

2. Equipment for the exam You are sure to have a question on fashion, so be prepared to draw fashion sketches. Have crayons or felt-tip colours with you. You may be allowed to use cut-out cardboard figures, about 6″ tall, to draw around, for your figure outlines.

3. Examination instructions, at the top of the paper, must be read very carefully. They may not be the same as in the old papers you have done in your "Mock" Exams. Make sure:
   How many questions you have to do.
   Which questions you **must** do.
   Which parts of the paper the questions must come from.

4. Planning your time The instructions may give you a quarter of an hour to read the paper, before you begin to write. Even if not, you should take that time to read and think about the **whole** paper. It is **not** a waste of time to think before you write.
   Look at each question in turn.
   Rule out any you know you cannot do.
   Try to see the point of each question—what is the examiner getting at?
   If you think an "essay" question needs only 2 or 3 sentences to answer it, then you must have missed the point of the question—avoid it.
   If you have, say, 1 hour 45 minutes for 3 questions, plan your time like this:

Reading the paper	15 minutes.
3 Questions, 25 minutes each	75 "
Reading through at the end	15 "
Total	105 minutes; or 1 hour, 45 minutes.

5. How many questions? If you have to do three, do **not** spend all your time on one, however much you know about it. You can get **only** one-third of the total marks for each question, so you **must** attempt all three.

6. How many parts to the question? Answer every part, unless the question gives you a choice. Suppose you have a

question like this, from the West Midlands C.S.E., 1969:

Question "(a) What do you understand by
(i) a facing
(ii) an interfacing?
(b) Give reasons for using interfacing in the making of garments.
(c) Give four examples where interfacing should be used.
(d) Explain fully how you would avoid bulk in the making of a garment. Illustrate this in the making of a round collar."

Ask yourself how the examiner might mark the parts of this question—probably out of 10:

Possible Marking

(a)	(i) What a facing **is**	1 mark.
	(ii) What an interfacing **is**	1 "
(b)	Why use it? Strength, stiffening	1 "
(c)	Four examples—collar, cuff, blouse front edge, waistband	4 "
(d)	Avoid bulk by layering, trimming seams, pressing darts open	2 "
	Illustrate round collar, showing V-shapes cut out of seam allowance, (as page 42)	1 "
	Total	10 marks.

This *may not* be the actual marking the examiner will use; but it shows how to break up a question, and make sure you leave nothing out.

7. Short-answer questions There may be a question in 20 or more parts, which says "Answer **briefly** each of the following:" This asks for an answer of one or two words, or at the most a sentence, for each part. **Do not** waste time writing an essay if you are asked: "Name four ways to control fullness."
The answer is simply: "Darts, Gathers, Pleats, Tucks." No more. If you cannot do **all** the parts, do what you can; but as they may carry only $\frac{1}{2}$ or $\frac{1}{4}$ mark each, do not spend a very long time over those you do not know.

8. Essay questions Make sure your answers **give information**. Do not write: "I should choose a skirt in a nice colour . . ." Instead, it would be better to write: "I should choose a warm brown, because it would tone with the cream blouse and tan cardigan I should wear with it; and it is a colour which suits my brown eyes and auburn hair." This tells the examiner that you know how to choose colours—"a nice colour" tells him nothing.
Answer the question as it is set, not as you would like it to be set. If asked: "How would you use a sewing machine to neaten seam edges?" Do **not** write about Overcasting, Loop-stitching or Herringboning, which are all done by hand. **Nor** should you try to write down everything you know about neatening.

Look at the exact wording of the question, and answer exactly that.

9. Fashion-drawing questions Do not be afraid of these questions, even if you cannot draw. They are marked for fashion sense, not for your drawing. Use cardboard figure cut-outs. Draw the outlines of the clothes lightly, and when you have settled all the details, use felt-tipped pens to draw a firm outline and to fill in colour. Be sure to show all the sewing details such as the placing of seams, darts, gathers, pockets, zip, belt, buttons, etc. Draw the back view if it is interesting or shows important details such as fastening. Show accessories. Describe the kind of fabric, the price, and the occasions for which you might wear the outfit.

10. Diagrams To show how different parts of a garment are made, should show only the details asked for in the question—do not make your diagrams messy by putting in too much. For instance, if you are asked to show the setting in of a sleeve, do not waste time drawing the cuff on the other end of the sleeve.
Draw your diagrams **large**. Remember that the examiner will be marking hundreds of papers, and diagrams the size of postage stamps are difficult to see—a good big diagram might well take up half the page, but the examiner will be grateful. Use words in the diagrams, specially to show the right and wrong sides of the fabric. Use arrows to point out any special details.

1. If you finish early First; sit back, close your eyes and relax for a minute. Then; read over your answers slowly, looking for faults of spelling or clumsy wording—try to put them right tidily. If you need to, you can add to an answer by putting a mark, "*—see page—" and adding a paragraph at the end of your answers.

12. The Practical Examination This exam is designed to test how well you can work, *quickly*. You will find that there is a great deal more to be done in 3 or $3\frac{1}{2}$ hours than you would think possible. In the planning period, when you can learn the pattern, make sure that you know exactly how to set about each part of it. Plan times for the different steps, and the order in which you will work.

For the exam itself, make sure that you are in the room as soon as you are allowed to be, so that you can get your machine threaded, and the stitch tried, before the exam begins.

Plan your time; for instance, suppose you have 3 hours to make up a sleeve with an opening and a cuff. Decide how much time you should spend on each step, like this:

Cut out fabric and interfacing. Make sure of Right and Left sides **now**. Later is too late	15 minutes.
Mark the fabric as necessary for what you need to do	10 „
Stay-stitch and cut the opening	5 „
Cut and tack on the continuous strip, and stitch	10 „
Press, trim; tack and hem the other edge	20 „
Stitch and neaten the sleeve seam	15 „
Gather the lower end of	

the sleeve; and the top end between the notches	15	,,
Tack and stitch the cuff, including the interfacing	15	,,
Layer and trim the raw edges, especially the corners. Turn and press	5	,,
Pin and tack sleeve to cuff and interfacing. Stitch	15	,,
Press. Hem down inner layer of cuff	10	,,
Work buttonhole. Sew on button	30	,,
Press	5	,,
Total	170	minutes,

(leaving 10 minutes spare.)

Save time by doing *at one time* as much pinning, or tacking, or machining as you can.

All this **can** be done in 3 hours, but there is no time to put right any mistakes you may make—so it is important not to rush into the work without thought. If you find that you are **not** going to finish, do not despair—few people **do** finish. But try to show at any rate *a little of everything*. For instance, if you have no time to finish the buttonhole or the hemming, at least **start** them and do a few stitches. The examiner will then have something to mark.

GOOD LUCK!

INDEX